T0112889

NAVIGATIONAL ENTANGLEMENTS

ALIETTE DE BODARD

TOR
DOT
COM

TOR PUBLISHING GROUP
NEW YORK

NAVIGATIONAL ENTANGLEMENTS

Copyright © 2024 by Aliette de Bodard

A Tordotcom Book
Published by Tom Doherty Associates / Tor Publishing Group
120 Broadway
New York, NY 10271

www.torpublishinggroup.com

Tor® is a registered trademark of Macmillan Publishing Group, LLC.

The Library of Congress Cataloging-in-Publication Data is available upon request.

ISBN 978-1-250-32488-7 (hardcover)
ISBN 978-1-250-79329-4 (ebook)

Our books may be purchased in bulk for promotional, educational, or business use. Please contact your local bookseller or the Macmillan Corporate and Premium Sales Department at 1-800-221-7945, extension 5442, or by email at MacmillanSpecialMarkets@macmillan.com.

First Edition: 2024

Printed in the United States of America

0 9 8 7 6 5 4 3 2 1

To my children, always and forever

NAVIGATIONAL
ENTANGLEMENTS

1

TANGLER CHASE

Việt Nhi had resigned herself, early on, to not liking people. And especially not people from the navigator clans. Which was more than a little unfortunate, as she was not just part of the navigator clans, but a Rooster disciple so junior that everyone could order her about into whatever fraught or difficult work needed to be done—and more often than not, said work included more contact with the clanspeople.

To wit, her current situation.

"There's been a . . . slight problem," Elder Mộng Liễu had said.

They were sitting in the reception hall of the Rooster fortress. In the background was the Central Needle and its steady flow of spaceships, rising—flashing golden for a moment as their navigators summoned their Shadows to cocoon them—and then vanishing into the Hollows, the space beyond the stars, beyond the void where travel went faster than light. Nhi liked being near the Needle: the dance of merchants boarding and ships lifting off was mesmerising and a comfort, a reassurance that the world was going on as it had always done.

She focused on the teacup in her hand, feeling its warmth against her skin. "What problem?" she asked.

"An incident with a ship."

"One of ours?"

Elder Liễu tightened her lips. "A Rat ship," she said.

Nhi tolerated Elder Liễu: she didn't equivocate, got straight to the point. And the only secret she had that Nhi could find was before she'd retired from active challenges in the void and stars circles—the society of navigators, always fighting each other for status—she'd loved an Ox navigator and passed on some minor information to him. Insofar as dark inner secrets went, it was tolerable.

She hadn't told that to Elder Liễu, of course. Most people didn't appreciate being told all of the truth, and Nhi couldn't always understand where the tipping point was between being honest and scaring off people. There were rules, but rules sometimes failed, because people were too messy. "We're not currently allied with the Rat clan," Nhi said, finally. She gripped her cup, finding solace in its smooth surface.

"No," Elder Liễu said. "But the imperials intervened." She raised a hand. "I know you hate politics, but the empire has requested we investigate."

All that Nhi understood of the empire was that it owned everything and that the merchants whose goods were transiting through the four major navigator clans owed allegiance to it. That was a good enough reason to say yes to whatever they suggested. "And you want me to investigate?" It made sense, because she was good at finding out things.

"No," Elder Liễu said. "I want you to deal with a tangler."

That stopped her. "A tangler? There's a tangler loose?"

Tanglers were large and tendriled creatures whose natural habitat was the Hollows—the space navigators took ships to, the space that enabled fast space travel. In their natural state, tanglers floated in the Hollows, grabbing other Hollows creatures and slowly digesting them. Unfortunately, this also included people travelling on ships, as tanglers fed on cognition: anyone human touched by their tendrils would gradually lose control over their own body, until death finally came as a mercy. And whenever a navigation gate was opened, there was a risk tanglers would go back to normal space, where they would prey on people.

A skillful navigator would use their Shadow to fend off tanglers, both during the navigation in the Hollows and during the opening and closing of navigation gates.

Clearly, something had gone wrong.

"Not just loose. Lost." Elder Liễu's face was grim. "It left the vicinity of the Rat Needle where the ship crashed, and it went . . . somewhere. We lost track of it."

"Somewhere." Nhi gripped her cup. A tangler loose outside the Hollows, where no one but the navigator clans could see them—tendrils trailing through streets and habitats, snaring people and draining them slowly of everything that made them sentient. She wasn't particularly scared of tanglers, but the idea offended her: tanglers belonged in the Hollows, not in the matter world.

"Who was the navigator?"

"A Rat called Phan Văn Đăng An."

"Ninth Judge," Nhi said. She couldn't place him, which meant she probably hadn't spent any extended period of time with him.

"I see your knowledge of clan business is still unparalleled," Elder Liễu said. It wasn't sarcasm, merely a statement of fact. She understood how Nhi worked.

"Well," Nhi said, still clutching her cup, "this Ninth Judge wasn't very good at what he was doing. His Shadow should have protected the ship." That was, after all, what Shadows were for.

"It didn't."

"And what about the protections at the Needle?"

"These failed, too."

"Those are serious failures." All navigators cultivated their own Shadow as part of their training: it was a physical extension of their khí, the life-energy that originated in the body's vitality center, low in the belly, and circulated along the body's network of meridians. Unfolded and projected outwards, their Shadow enabled them to open gates to the Hollows, and to keep their ships whole during the transit— both against the pressures of the Hollows themselves, and against tanglers. It also enabled them to fight other navigators, whether in the Hollows or outside them, the usual way hierarchy was established among the clans. Every clan— and every teacher in every clan—had a different style of Shadow. Ninth Judge's Shadow should have turned the tangler aside, and if that failed, the Needles in the various clan-controlled spaceports were heavily protected, to make sure that tanglers emerging from the Hollows into the matter world would be contained, and sent back to the Hollows. Nhi could see why the empire was unhappy. "You said the tangler went somewhere. Into imperial space?" Nhi asked.

A shrug, from Elder Liễu. "I don't know," she said. "But yes, that's the suspicion."

Clans controlled their own fortress and their central Needles, and the lesser Needles and associated spaceports in their own networks. The empire controlled the rest. "I'm not the best person for this," she said.

Low laughter, from Elder Liễu. "And coming from you, it's not false humility, is it. Just a statement of fact."

Nhi was flagging. This conversation was too unpredictable, and her small reserves of energy were starting to get depleted. She summoned her Shadow, felt it rise, trembling, from her vitality center, and spread through her meridians, a warm, golden flow of power—like being under heavy rocks, a grip that held and comforted her. Her full Shadow would be golden wings and thick veils of energy: Nhi's style, the Heavenly Weave, was ponderous and powerful, unlike Elder Liễu's own, more aggressive Blood-Extinguishing Palm. "I advise you to send someone else," Nhi said.

A grimace from Elder Liễu, which Nhi knew was bad news. It meant whatever she asked for wasn't convenient. "I don't have someone else. And—" She paused, and again that grimace on her face. Nhi gripped her Shadow more tightly. "The empire has asked for a delegation of major clans. They are annoyed with us. They want the tangler caught before more deaths can occur."

Nhi could understand that—she'd be annoyed, too, if something so large had gone wrong. But, still . . . "Elder—"

"You'll be our delegate," Elder Liễu said, firmly. "Meanwhile, we'll be investigating the matter of the crash with the other elders from the major clans."

"I'd rather not do this," Nhi said, knowing already that it was pointless.

"I'm afraid we don't always do the things we like," Elder Liễu said, slowly, smoothly.

Insofar as Nhi was concerned, she *never* got to do the things she liked. Too much noise, too many people—and she'd much rather stay in the Rooster fortress cultivating, but the way things were structured there made it extremely hard. She was meant to go out and make a name for herself—to grow old without being killed by some other clan's navigator, whether major or minor. To prove herself. And knowing far too much about people didn't help with that—what the clans respected was defeating other navigators and transporting large ships safely. But to do the latter, one had to first do the former.

Elder Liễu said, "I believe the other clans sent people you'll be familiar with. That means you should be able to work together."

Nhi tried to smile. It was probably coming off as insincere, but Elder Liễu respected the attempt rather than the content.

"I'll go," she said.

"Good," Elder Liễu said. "The imperial envoy, Ly Châu, is arriving at the Rooster Needle. You can go and wait for her with the others."

The others. The others were already here. Nhi fought a brief moment of panic: things were happening too fast, too uncontrollably. She released her Shadow—feeling the loss of security keenly—and tried to look forward to the mission. An utter failure. This was dangerous, and had far too much uncertainty.

And, worse, it had people. Not just any people: Nhi was going to have to put up with her *peers*.

All too soon, Nhi found herself in a lineup of far too many people, waiting for a ship to emerge from the Hollows.

She'd usually have dressed in flamboyant finery like armour, but Elder Liễu had ushered Nhi straight from her quarters onto the landing platform. It was the largest one at the Needle, the one nearest to the ground floor. Like all platforms, it was surrounded on all sides by various buildings where clan members would store supplies as well as renew the protections around the landing area itself. Its portico, nearest to the Needle, was now filled with most of the dignitaries of the Rooster clan: too many people, too much noise, and the expectation that Nhi would have to make small talk—which she hated at the best of times and certainly couldn't keep up with the stress eating at her innards.

Elder Liễu led Nhi to a place near the front, where the flamboyant colors of the Roosters gave way to the more subdued ones of other clans. Nhi clung to her unfolded Shadow, trying to steer through the din of sounds and the closeness of other people as much as she could.

Ahead of the clan's Shadow protections—a pressure Nhi could feel getting stronger and stronger, turning the air to tar—two people were waiting, wearing the robes of juniors.

"These are the delegates from the other clans. Everyone bar the Rat envoy, who's already with the imperial envoy," Elder Liễu said. "Children, this is Nhi."

Two pairs of eyes turned to stare at Nhi—who felt herself withering under the weight of the combined attention.

"Ah, the Rooster. I'm Hạc Cúc." Hạc Cúc looked to be in

her midtwenties—old, for a junior. She had a sharp, edged face and an impeccable topknot. She moved brashly and confidently; she appeared present in every movement, every toss of her head and shrug of her shoulders. Nhi had a vague memory of her from clan gatherings fifteen or so years ago—as a standoffish child whose respect for rules was likely to get peers into trouble. There was nothing of that here now: she was magnetic and at the same time almost too much, like a sun pulling you into its orbit before you'd realized what would happen.

"Honoured to meet you," she said.

A sharp look from Hạc Cúc. "Mmm. Pleased to be here?" The Snakes kept order among themselves, and among the clans. Their pragmatic and brutal assassinations of rules-breakers were well-known. Hạc Cúc wore the clothes of an enforcer, and moved like one. Probably not to be crossed if one was sensible, and if one didn't wish to wake up poisoned, or with a gun wound to the chest, or any of the myriad ways the Snakes had of dispatching their victims.

Not that Nhi was sensible when it came to her own duties, or keeping her own given word. She plastered her brightest and most pointed smile on her face. "I go where my clan needs me."

Hạc Cúc smiled, and said nothing more.

"Hello, em." The Ox envoy was Lành, an older woman in her thirties, wearing gloves to hide the minute scars on her hands. Nhi knew her; they'd worked together before. Lành had been the only survivor of a crash involving tanglers, an unheard-of occurrence that had brought her fame as a child, a fame that hadn't carried into adulthood. Lành was weird, bitter, abrasive, but Nhi found her restful; she was frank, and her actions were easy to predict. "Good to see you here."

Nhi laughed, sharply. "Let's see what's good, eh."

Lành smiled, a rare enough expression from her. Next to her, Hạc Cúc looked as if she'd swallowed something sour. "Not this company," she said, sharply.

It couldn't be Nhi who was the issue, so it had to be Lành. Great. It wasn't just going to be a mission where Nhi had to deal with people, but a mission where she was going to have to prevent people from killing each other.

"You know her?" Nhi asked Lành, in a whisper.

"Shh," Elder Liễu said. "Incoming ship."

The air tightened. Nhi unfolded her own Shadow—and felt the pressure of other Shadows in the courtyard, every navigator unfolding theirs as a precaution against tanglers. But the bulk of the pressure wasn't other Shadows: it felt as though everything was tearing itself apart—as if only an act of Heaven kept them all from being torn into fragments. Nhi's Shadow fluttered, caught in the grip of the gate. Even behind layers and layers of clan protection, the pull of that gate—the pull of the Hollows—was almost too much.

A hole appeared in the center of the courtyard, filled with shimmering iridescence halfway between pearl and oil, which then became pinpoints of lights, like distant stars, except those lights kept shifting and distorting. Inside were the Hollows: the darkness where they navigated, where the tanglers were born and lived and died. Outside, on the edges, the air was roiling and roiling like a storm, Shadow bursting into the center, cleaved into myriad fragments.

Something pushed through, and the air burst like a series of bubbles. Nhi's ears ached, and her arms shook with the pressure of keeping herself upright. Everyone in the courtyard looked various degrees of uncomfortable; gates always had that effect. If not for the necessity of welcoming the imperial envoy, no one would have been out there.

The imperial ship was small—the size of the room where Elder Liễu had welcomed Nhi, and like the room it was bulky, imposing, all straight angles and weaponry ports, and generally looked like something from two or three generations back of ships. The clans had moved on to sleeker things, but the empire much preferred to go for reliable and intimidating. It glistened as it came out of the Hollows—some of that iridescence clinging to it and cascading into the courtyard like a flare of ashes from an explosion. Then the gate shut, and the ship landed in the middle of the courtyard.

Nhi breathed out at the same time as everyone else. The uncanny pressure on her Shadow was gone, but she didn't dare to let go. It was Elder Liễu who gestured her forward at the same time as the ship extended a steel gangplank towards the ground, and two people appeared framed in its opening. "Kneel," Elder Liễu said. "As we honour the empire."

Nhi knelt, head bowed. So did the other two juniors, and Elder Liễu. The rest of the clan pointedly did not. A barbed, edged honouring.

Footsteps, on the gangplank. Slow and steady. A shape getting closer and closer. With her head bowed, all Nhi could see was the hem of a richly embroidered tunic—brown and red, the colors of the Dog clan—fluttering in the breeze from the recently closed navigation gate.

"So," a voice said. "These are my clan delegates." Ly Châu, the imperial envoy.

"Your Honour," Elder Liễu said.

Ly Châu's voice, sarcastic and annoyed, cut her off. "Such an honour. Get up," she said, sharply, to the juniors.

They scrambled up, not daring to look up. When they finally did, they saw a woman of slim build, with a young face and a topknot kept together by glittering silver pins. She was tapping a steel fan against her gloved left hand and scowling, looking as if she'd just found something unpleasant under her shoes.

Two attendants scurried by, holding out a tray with teacups. Ly Châu took one and drained it in one gulp, setting it back on the table with barely a second look. She didn't move to sit or serve anyone else.

"Snake," Ly Châu said. She stared at Hạc Cúc, who was showing her the proper respect by averting her gaze. "You look underfed. Can you even carry your own weight around?"

Hạc Cúc's face did not move, but her whole body tensed.

"Ox," Ly Châu said to Lành. "Or is it tangler?"

Lành colored. Everyone in the clans knew that she'd been the sole survivor of a tangler attack, that her Shadow was sometimes a little too odd and too uncanny.

"Leave her alone," Nhi said, sharply. She knew it wasn't the smartest thing to speak up, but Ly Châu's casual humiliation was too much to bear.

"Oh, a Rooster with a sense of justice? That'd be a first," Ly Châu said. "You people usually care more about your finery and your fights."

Nhi's hands bunched into fists. "I thought we were here to chase a tangler," she said.

"A tangler you lot let escape?" Ly Châu smiled. She gestured; behind her was a second person wearing the tunic of the Rat clan, a young woman who was wrapped in her own Shadow and doing her best to fade into the background. Nhi didn't blame her, if she'd had to put up with Ly Châu for long. "This is Bảo Duy, from the Rats. She's been some help on this." The way she said "some" clearly said Bảo Duy had come up short of all her low expectations.

Bảo Duy gave Hạc Cúc and Nhi a curt nod. She looked haggard and stressed. Nhi struggled to remember what she knew about her. The name was vaguely familiar, but Nhi would look it up when she wasn't already struggling to keep herself together. She'd also need to look up Hạc Cúc, about whom she only had vague memories. She needed information. She needed secrets. Something she could hold to keep things under control.

Elder Liễu said, "I trust these are acceptable?"

Ly Châu looked thoughtful. For a moment Nhi fantasized she was going to say no, that she'd get to go back to her rooms and her tranquility. "The best the clans can send," Ly Châu drawled.

Elder Liễu's face was neutral. "Of course. Did you doubt it?"

"Never for a moment," Ly Châu said. Her smile was predatory. "You know exactly in what regard I hold you."

Ouch. Elder Liễu didn't flinch, but Nhi did.

"Come," Ly Châu said, to the juniors. She held out her fan to Hạc Cúc, as if she were a low-level servant. "You can hold that. Snake."

Nhi didn't dare to look at Hạc Cúc's face: an elite assassin ordered about with utter contempt. At last, Hạc Cúc unfolded, grabbing the fan with a little too much speed and roughness. "It's my honour," she said, sourly.

"Come on," Ly Châu said. "The hour grows late, and we're not going to tarry here."

It was a slap in the face: a quick turnaround, with just that single teacup drunk, and nothing shared with the Roosters. Yes, there was a tangler loose, but there were also rules of etiquette. Ly Châu was effectively saying the entire Rooster clan wasn't worth her attention.

Lành straightened up and gave Ly Châu a resigned look, and then bowed, very deeply and respectfully, before following Hạc Cúc onto the ship. Ah. Making the best of a bad situation.

That had never been Nhi's style.

"Your Excellency," Nhi said.

A raised eyebrow, from Ly Châu. The honorific was overboard: Nhi had used it because she guessed Ly Châu wanted to be respected beyond what she deserved. By Ly Châu's taut face, Nhi had guessed wrong.

"Are we not going to stay—" Nhi stopped then, because Elder Liễu had grabbed her by the wrist, a shock. Nhi didn't like to be touched; she froze, words drying up.

"We'll look forward to hearing from you," Elder Liễu said, smoothly and carefully. She gave Nhi's wrist a gentle push, ushering her towards the gangplank. "As you keep us all safe."

Nhi took a deep breath and followed Lành into the shadowed interior. Ly Châu and Bảo Duy came in, and Ly Châu gestured for all of them to stand together. She looked at them, thoughtfully, as the gangplank lifted and the door closed—and her Shadow grew, enfolding the ship, ready to open a navigation gate again.

"What am I going to do with you," she said. It wasn't even sharp or malicious. Just matter-of-factly disappointed. "Well, I guess I'll figure something out." And she turned away from them to go into the control room.

Hạc Cúc set the fan on one of the benches near the opening. "I already hate all of this," she said. She sounded annoyed. "Please tell me it gets better."

Bảo Duy, the Rat, who'd been silent till then, said with a very heartfelt sigh, "She's always like this. Or worse."

"Great," Hạc Cúc muttered. She looked as though she wanted to stab someone.

Lành said, "We're just going to have to put up with her until she's gone."

"Fawn over Ly Châu. How exactly like you," Hạc Cúc said, and matters might have turned sour if Nhi hadn't intervened.

"Let's go see our bunks on this ship," she said, bright and forced. "Bảo Duy, where do you sleep?"

Bảo Duy took the lead, obviously relieved at having to provide expert facts—as opposed to navigating clan politics, or getting on in any way, shape, or form with other juniors from other clans.

And, just like that, they were on their own—not just on a tangler hunt, but with the prospect of days and months on board a ship with someone who despised them all.

It was going to be a miracle if it went well. If any of it went well.

Hạc Cúc usually liked people, for short periods of time—usually before she poisoned or stabbed them as part of her job for the Snake clan.

At the moment, she was charming a waiter in a small wayhouse. The wayhouse was in the center of the Silver Stream, a string of asteroids that trailed around the Ice Jade Planet that had once made up its now fractured moon. On one of the largest Fragments, a city of buildings clinging to rock faces had sprung into existence: a chaotic place, where no two building clusters had the same orientation.

The Silver Stream was on the edge of imperial-controlled space. Usually, as a Snake clan member, Hạc Cúc would be careful who she charmed—even more so if she had to harm or kill them. But she and the other juniors were with the imperial envoy, weren't they? Blessed by her presence, small saplings sheltering beneath the canopy of her grace. Which made it acceptable to . . . let loose. Be less careful, more aggressive.

Chasing a lost tangler sounded like a lot of time wasting. It was a thankless group effort for which all the credit would go to Ly Châu, the Dog envoy. "So there have been no odd sightings?" she asked. She itched to get back to *The Steel Clam,* her own ship, her own passengers. She was wasting opportunities down there.

The waiter—young, muscular—set down the tea on the table, in a place well-connected to the energy-founts, which drew power from the Fragment's mantle. Hạc Cúc watched as the energy flowed from the fount to the kettle, over the network of shining blue across the metal floor—the paths set by the masters of wind and water. It would keep the water at the right temperature for several brews. A pity she wasn't planning to be around for most of them.

"What do you mean by odd sightings?" the waiter asked.

"People going missing," Hạc Cúc asked. "Or people coming back odd." The body of a tangler was large and visible, but the tendrils were long: they could spread for measures, easily three to five times as long as a ship. The tendrils couldn't be seen. Any light that hit them was refracted in a part of the spectrum beyond what most people's eyes could see. They would get hurt long before they saw anything. Hạc Cúc deliberately didn't mention anything further; no need to alert the general population.

The waiter gestured to the narrow opening of the wayhouse, through which Hạc Cúc could see a ballet of small shuttles going from cluster to cluster—to hydroponics farms, founts-network maintenance, comms, teahouses, restaurants . . . "It's a spread-out place. Hard to know if people are going missing." But he looked away from her, and Hạc Cúc could tell he was thinking.

"Tell me," she said.

"People go to the Old Rise." He seemed to realize, suddenly, that he'd said something he shouldn't, and clammed up.

"The Old Rise." Hạc Cúc chewed on it for a while. In the areas around Needles, people trafficked in all sorts of things, and especially those Needles on the border between clan-controlled space and imperial-controlled space. She smiled. "I'm not empire." She gestured, her clothes shifting to display the insignia of the Snake clan.

She hadn't expected it to put him at ease. Snakes had a reputation in the void and stars circles, and outside of it, too. Pragmatic, stealthy, ruthless. Also just, but most people saw the bloodthirstiness of the retribution rather than the upholding of the rules.

The waiter swallowed, shaking.

"I'm not here for you," Hạc Cúc said, lightly. "Or for whatever borderline-legal commerce you have. I don't follow the rules of the empire or care much for them."

He lowered his gaze, as if he was going to throw himself to the floor in the traditional gesture of respect. Hạc Cúc summoned her Shadow—moving fast and unseen, putting a hand under his chin and holding him upright. "And not here for you to abase yourself, either," she said, mildly. She could feel his heartbeat pulsing through the golden glow of her Shadow, magnified ten thousand times. "What's happening at the Old Rise?"

He struggled in her grasp, but not much. Hạc Cúc held him for a few more moments, pressing lightly on his windpipe—just enough to remind him she could crush it. And she would, too: there were too many lives at stake if they didn't find the tangler. That she hated the mission with a passion didn't mean she wasn't going to do it well.

"Please—" he said.

Hạc Cúc set him down. Not one of the customers in the wayhouse had moved. They were looking towards the opening, wondering when it would be safe to leave. "So?"

"I'm—" The waiter struggled to get his voice under control. "I'm not sure. But you asked about people disappearing, and Old Madam Hậu and her children went there and didn't come back."

"How long ago?"

"It was three days."

Hmm. Was it worth checking? Time would tell. "I see," Hạc Cúc said. "Thank you." She folded her Shadow. Then she sat down again, poured the hot water over the leaves in the teapot, and brewed them, mentally counting time—heedless of the way people were scurrying away from the shop. He wouldn't call the militia—and even if he did, nothing was going to happen.

She inhaled the aroma of the tea: it was Fish Hook, smelling of brine on a faraway planet.

Perfect.

A ping, from her personal comms device. It was Ly Châu. "Little Miss Snake," she said, icily. "I didn't give you permission to traipse around the Fragments whenever you felt like it. Come back to the inn now."

Hạc Cúc considered not answering, but her sư phụ had drilled manners into her—specifically, that there was no use antagonizing a powerful opponent before it was needful. But Ancestors in Heaven, how she hated the woman. "As you wish, Your Excellency," she said. She used one of the pronouns for an official far above her station—a borderline insult, as Ly Châu would know exactly.

Ly Châu didn't answer.

Ly Châu was also conspicuously absent from the common room of their inn by the time Hạc Cúc made her way back to it; she'd taken the long way around, waiting for common shuttles rather than hiring a private one. Her initial satisfaction at getting the information from the waiter had faded: it was too little and too inconclusive, and she'd kept hearing her sư phụ's voice in her head, telling her that violence was to be used with intent and purpose. If he'd been there, he'd have gotten more, even if he'd had to threaten all the customers in the wayhouse. He wouldn't be left with a vague place name, and the name of a missing person far too common to locate.

"Look who's there," Lành said. "The prodigal."

Lành was the Ox junior: mousy and trembling and always looking like she wanted to disappear into the walls or the floor. Hạc Cúc knew her; they'd hated each other for ten years now. "The tangler friend," Hạc Cúc said, sitting down and drawing a bowl of noodles to her from the heating plate in the center of the table. She couldn't see Việt Nhi, the Rooster junior, anywhere; she was probably reading a book in the room they all shared.

At this hour of the night, the room was busy, but not overly so. It was a large, square space, its energy coming from the center of the room. Blue lines snaked from three energy-founts to the heating plates in the center of each table, and the tables themselves were carved steel worked to mimic wood, a different quote from a revered scholar carved into each table. The customers were mostly merchants and business travelers, and everyone ate while paying studious non-attention to the juniors, who obviously—from their accent to the utilitarian cut of their clothes—were clan.

No one liked to interfere in clan business, and they would even less like to interfere with Ly Châu—who wore the brown and red of the Dog clan proudly and looked as though any moment she was going to arrest everyone for violation of the law.

"Can we just *try* to get on with each other?" Bảo Duy,

the Rat junior, asked. She was thin and had large, percep-
tive eyes; she moved too much and too fast, as if her body
couldn't quite keep up with the speed of her thoughts. Hạc
Cúc didn't know her and hadn't been terribly impressed. If
nothing else, it was her clan's fault that they were all here.

"If she stops referring to me as tangler friend," Lành
said. "Which I'm not."

Hạc Cúc snorted. "You started this one."

"I'm not the one who's failing to follow orders," Lành
said, viciously. "How are you ever going to live up to your
sư phụ's reputation if you can't follow simple instructions?"
Her Shadow came into focus around her, pulsing with unfamiliar and dark reflections that looked far too much like
tangler trails in the Hollows.

Hạc Cúc saw red. "Take it back," she snapped. She held
both chopsticks, poised to throw them at Lành—she didn't
summon her own Shadow, but it took an effort.

Lành raised an eyebrow. "Or what? Are you going to
take me down? That'll make a pretty mess for Ly Châu to
sort out."

"No one is going to take anyone down," Bảo Duy
snapped, irritably. "I can't believe I'm having to be the adult
here. Stop it. Now."

*Kinder, little fish. You have to be kinder. You don't know
what Lành has been through,* Hạc Cúc's sư phụ had said, over
and over.

And she did know. She did know that a tangler attack
had wiped out Lành's family and a good part of the Ox clan
when she was a child. She knew that, if her sư phụ hadn't
been there, Lành would be dead. She did know, and she
was trying.

And it wasn't even the Shadow—though the appearance, the slimy feel of it, too reminiscent of that taut feeling before a tangler attack in the Hollows, set Hạc Cúc on edge. It was the fact that Lành always deferred to the strongest. She had no morals, no principles.

Kinder. Be kinder.

Lành was right, wasn't she? She'd never be worthy of her sư phụ. Never be respected or loved, because she'd failed.

A hand, on her shoulder. Hạc Cúc turned, whiplash fast, the chopsticks leaving her hands—and the person behind her didn't move, but the chopsticks bounced against Shadow, a thick veil that deflected them.

They hit the floor, the sound of their fall ringing in the sudden silence.

Hạc Cúc stared at the person: it was Nhi, the Rooster junior who'd been mostly avoiding the company, a broad, sarcastic smile on her face. "Chopsticks make terribly inefficient weapons," she said.

She was tall, gangly, and seemingly awkward, but there had been nothing awkward about the way she'd deflected the chopsticks. She had an impeccable topknot, unlike Hạc Cúc's own. Her eyes were small, her nose and thin lips sharp in a moon-shaped, round face. Said lips were now thinner, closed into something very much like a disparaging smile.

Hạc Cúc clenched her fists; the tone had been a mere statement of fact, but the facts hurt.

Lành stared at Nhi. "Don't interfere."

"Why not?" Nhi asked.

"This is between us."

Nhi huffed. Her Shadow was visible now: slow and

ponderous. Hạc Cúc couldn't remember which style of navigation she practiced, but it looked to be defensive rather than offensive. "I'm sure that'll be a terrific thing to tell Ly Châu when she comes back and finds out two of us have killed each other."

"I wouldn't kill her!"

"Oh. So good to know," Nhi said. Her hand was still on Hạc Cúc's shoulder: a grip of iron. "What about you?"

Be kinder.

She wasn't kind. She was prickly and aggressive, an enforcer, but never the respected navigator her sư phụ was. A failure. "I can be convinced to let it go," she said, gritting her teeth.

"Good." Nhi stared at Lành—who held her Shadow a while longer—long enough for Hạc Cúc to force her breathing under control.

"Fine," Lành said, and dropped it. "She makes an effort, I make an effort."

"How did you even show up?" Hạc Cúc asked.

"I was trying to read in the corner," Nhi said. "A doomed effort, I now see." She smiled at Lành. It was all sharp teeth, and suddenly Hạc Cúc saw why Nhi had been avoiding them. It was because she didn't care enough about any of them. Roosters were flamboyant and aggressive, and Nhi had seemed so out of character for one—but it was just because she'd thought them all beneath her notice.

That *hurt.*

"Well," Hạc Cúc said, brightly, with a cheerfulness she had to fake, "we're done now. You can go back to your reading."

Nhi's hand lingered an instant longer on her shoulder;

she was looking at Hạc Cúc as if assessing her. "Phạm Thị Hạc Cúc," she said, thoughtfully. "You practice Divine Harmony. They say you're the fastest navigator of your generation. Student of the Pure Heart Master Quang Lộc. Blade of the Redwood Star."

Hạc Cúc lifted Nhi's hand from her shoulder, glaring at her. "Titles are *earned*," she said, icily. "Which isn't where I am yet."

Nhi stared back. Most people would have been afraid, but she wasn't, not one bit. But not because of any anger or desire to hurt, the way Lành had been; she was merely taking in facts and chewing on them. "Good to know," she said. "I'm sure there will be opportunities on this trip." She raised her other hand. "Here. Your chopsticks."

Hạc Cúc sat down, unsure what to think about what had just happened. She settled for glaring at her noodle soup, always a surefire way to handle problems—and jabbed her chopsticks into the bowl the way she would have driven a knife into someone's chest. "Opportunities," she said, tasting the oddness of her own words. "Opportunities."

When Ly Châu still didn't appear the following morning at breakfast, there was a moment of uncertainty.

Hạc Cúc caught Nhi's eye. "Maybe we should check," she said.

It took a little charm from Hạc Cúc to convince the inn's owner to give them the safety override for the lock in Ly Châu's room—and a little more arguing between Lành and Hạc Cúc before they all agreed to go to the room.

Nhi threw open the door. "Your Honor?" she said. "Your Honor?"

Hạc Cúc had stepped a little deeper into the room. "No need," she said, bleakly.

Nhi hadn't *liked* Ly Châu. She was overbearing and controlling, and she'd enjoyed bossing them around far too much. And the four juniors might have quarreled about many things—about most things, really, insofar as Lành and Hạc Cúc were concerned—but they'd all agreed she was a terrible person, and they couldn't wait for the mission to be over so they could be rid of them.

It was, therefore, both terribly appropriate and terribly unfortunate when they found that Ly Châu was lying on the bed, dead.

Bảo Duy was kneeling by the side of the corpse, taking the pulse, heedless of the quarrel. "Nebula Cinnabar," she said, quietly.

That much was obvious: nothing else left such traces— the revulsed lips, the blue extremities, the particular vacancy in the eyes. The issue was that Nebula Cinnabar was a clan poison; anyone outside the clan would have a hard time accessing it.

What had happened here, and why?

This was a disaster.

"You should have kept a better eye on her," Hạc Cúc said.

Lành reeled as if struck. "I—?"

"You're the one who was ingratiating yourself with her." Lành had decided to deal with the problem of Ly Châu by being at her beck and call, a fact that had annoyed Hạc Cúc even more. Nhi didn't really blame Lành for that; it had been hard enough on board that small ship, being sent right and left on trivial errands, and mocked at every turn.

But clearly, every disaster could be made infinitely

worse. Nhi sighed, inwardly. It was probably left to her to solve this one, and she only had one way of solving quarrels: the truth, which tended to set everyone at her own throat. "You're compensating, aren't you?"

Hạc Cúc drew herself to her full height, Shadow trembling around her in a variegated halo. "What are you insinuating?"

"For not being the one who ended her. You're Snake," Nhi said, curtly. "Assassination is your specialty, isn't it? Rather frustrating to find someone beat you to it." Nhi's forage into the network had confirmed Hạc Cúc worked as an assassin for her clan, and that her devotion to her art had estranged her from her peers. Pride in her abilities would be a sensitive spot.

Hạc Cúc turned an interesting shade of red—but then she frowned. "Are you trying to annoy me so much I give up on blaming Lành and turn my attention to you?"

Nhi, in spite of herself, laughed. She'd expected anger, not this amused self-awareness. "Please grant me your attention, o bà." She used a pronoun for people much older or much higher in the hierarchy, deliberately inappropriate.

Hạc Cúc stared at her, at the corpse, and then around the room. "No sign of forced entry," she said.

"No," Nhi said. "The lock was untouched, and the owner made such difficulty giving us the overrides, it's not likely that they would have given them to anyone else."

"Unless it's one of us," Hạc Cúc said.

"Why would we—" It was Lành.

Hạc Cúc ignored her.

"Can't be one of us," Nhi said. The speed with which this was happening was exhilarating.

"No," Hạc Cúc said, almost at the same time. "We've been with her for a few days now. We'd have done it earlier. And probably while she had us out trying to find tangler tracks."

"And if it's not us—"

"Someone who hates the empire?" Hạc Cúc asked.

"Mmm. Possible. She was out yesterday," Nhi said. Ly Châu kept secrets; of course she did. The first and most obvious was how insecure she was, how unsteady in her own power. But perhaps there were deeper ones. Perhaps this was why she had been killed. Nhi felt a thrill in her bones, in her unmaterialized Shadow, at the thought of digging deeper. Of finding out what had been hidden, dragging it into the light. "Perhaps she was poisoned then."

"Nebula Cinnabar is a slow poison," Hạc Cúc said, with the authoritativeness of a Snake.

"How slow?"

"Slow enough that she didn't need to be poisoned yesterday."

Nhi stared at her, and then at Lành, who'd moved closer to the exit. Bảo Duy had finished examining the corpse. Some utterly alien urge came to Nhi: she didn't want this conversation with Hạc Cúc—this unfamiliar experience that sent a thrill into her bones—to end.

"What did you find?" she asked Bảo Duy.

Bảo Duy shrugged. "Traces of Shadow. She got into a fight at some point. Maybe before she entered the room. They're too faint for me to work out more information."

A pity. Each navigator clan had its own specific way of handling Shadow, and within each clan, each lineage under one sư phụ its own style. It could have been quite useful, if it had panned out.

"Em," Nhi said to Lành and Bảo Duy. "Can you find out where she went yesterday and if anyone visited her?" she asked. "Hạc Cúc and I will search the room further."

Bảo Duy looked at her and Hạc Cúc. "The Roosters weren't left in charge of anyone, least of all other major clans."

"Oh, come on," Lành said, drawling. "Do you want to stay here with such company?"

Nhi moved closer to Hạc Cúc, laid a hand on her as she made a visible effort to control herself. Then, softly, into her ear, "Please don't say anything. I'm trying to help you." It felt strangely transgressive; she was never this close to people usually. She could feel her own breath, hot and humid, in the air between them.

Bảo Duy and Lành left, and the door closed behind them. It felt like an eternity.

Hạc Cúc shook herself away from Nhi, and glared at her. "I don't need help," she said, acidly. "And even less charity."

Nhi was used to people getting upset with her, and when it was strangers it didn't faze her. It was a fact of her life so far that eventually she would say the things that were true but that people didn't want to hear, and that then, at best, they would leave. Or get angry. "Good to know," she said. "Why Lành?"

"Why what?"

"You keep picking quarrels with her," Nhi said. "Because you think her too accommodating?"

Hạc Cúc looked surprised. "That's the question you're

asking me?" She gestured towards the bed. "We should have other priorities."

Nhi said, "No, I want to know."

A soft, disbelieving snort from Hạc Cúc. "You're something else." But it wasn't aggressive anymore. "Lành bows to anyone who looks decisive or strong enough."

"But not to you." Was it power? Nhi was used to that answer, and it would make sense.

"One doesn't bow to anyone," Hạc Cúc said. "Only to higher principles. You don't compromise on morals because someone is stronger than you."

Ah. She was following the ideals of the Snake clan, then: justice above all else. "What does it matter to you?" Hạc Cúc asked. She crossed her fingers, leaning against the wall. "I've heard of you, Việt Nhi. The outcast in the Rooster clan. The one who'd rather be left alone. A bit troublesome when your clan's way of life involves so much . . . contact."

Nhi was being dissected as effectively as a specimen on a steel table. It should have been unpleasant, but Hạc Cúc's voice was utterly matter-of-fact, without aggression. Just trying to puzzle out something, and it was something Nhi could understand, that drive to take people apart, to make them make sense when they so seldom did. Above all, it made her feel *seen*, and it was an unsettling feeling that left a tight warmth in her belly. "I like secrets," she said.

Other people she'd said this to usually became hostile, or profoundly misunderstood. But Hạc Cúc just stared at her, for a while. "Ah," she said, finally. Her demeanor softened. "Because they make sense, don't they? You feel you finally have an advantage because you know what moves us. How we might react in a given situation."

Nhi felt as though the breath had been stolen from her. "Yes," she said.

Hạc Cúc nodded, briskly. "Let's look at that corpse, shall we?" She held out her hand. Nhi didn't dare take it, but she did move closer.

The room was the same as the one the juniors shared, except smaller: the energy-fount in a corner, everything else arranged to let the energy flow freely to the bed and the light above it. The window-screen, connected to the Silver Stream's network, displayed a rotating selection of nearby building clusters; the current one was a large one, buildings on either side of a deep chasm.

A small tea kettle was on the table. It had been moved away from the flow. Nhi stared at the tea for a while. She wasn't sure why, but she reached out and put the kettle back on the flow. A blue line snapped into being between the energy-fount and the kettle, and a faint whistle came from the water inside.

"Old leaves," Hạc Cúc said, behind her. "More than a day old. She didn't drink any tea yesterday."

"Mmm," Nhi said.

Hạc Cúc was staring at the body with the expert eye of someone whose business involved a lot of contact with them. Nhi didn't like fresh corpses; they were troubling, something that didn't quite follow her unspoken rules. They looked alive, but small details weren't quite right: the sallowness of the skin, the lack of breathing, the way energy flows would just dead-end into them.

She focused instead on the room. The floor had recon-figured itself with the new distribution of energy flows after she'd put the kettle back on. There was something . . . She called up her Shadow—felt it rise around her, ponderous and crushing. With her Heavenly Weave powers close to her, she could see what had eluded her. "Tangler," she said, softly.

Hạc Cúc looked up, sharply. "If there was a tangler's tendril in this room, we'd all be stung." And it wasn't like they could miss it; even a small hit would make it harder for people to summon their Shadow. Lành was the only person who'd ever survived being in prolonged contact with tanglers, and even Nhi had to admit it had made her absolutely odd.

"It was there," Nhi said. A faint line, bisecting the room from the furthest wall to the bed. Odd. Why had it gone through the walls? She mentally traced the line. Hạc Cúc was right: if this was a tendril, it'd have gone through half the inn, including the room where the juniors were sleeping together. Or squabbling together, at any given time.

Hạc Cúc whistled through her teeth. "She *was* stung," she said. "Look at the hands."

"I'd rather not," Nhi said. "I don't like corpses." She braced herself for an argument, but instead Hạc Cúc nodded.

"Abraded," Hạc Cúc said, curtly. "Multiple times."

"She kept running into obstacles?"

"Yes."

Loss of depth perception, then. That was bad. "I don't understand how it all comes together; I'm not an expert in tanglers. But Bảo Duy is."

"She is." A sigh, from Hạc Cúc. "So is Lành."

Nhi winced at the thought. She'd asked Lành about Hạc Cúc, and the Ox had simply said "Stay away from her" in a way that brooked no argument. Clearly, the dislike for each other was mutual. Nhi wasn't idealistic enough to think she could fix anything between them. Lành clearly didn't need any help, and would only get offended if Nhi interfered. "Let's not ask Lành right away, shall we?"

Soft laughter, from Hạc Cúc. She'd moved away from the body, came to stand by Nhi's side. "I appreciate the thought, but as I told you, I don't need the help. Ly Châu is dead; we need to find that tangler, and her murderer. That's a lot for four juniors who don't get on, and even more so if Lành and I continue at each other's throats."

She was relaxed now, and there was something about her that just drew Nhi's gaze and held it. Not the face—sharp and angular, the eyes deeply recessed into it, the hair sweeping back—but a sense of presence, of investment in the then and now. Absolute belief in what was right and what wasn't. It was . . . oddly magnetic.

"We should tell the elders," Nhi said.

Hạc Cúc made a face. "The nearest Needle is not that far. It's downworld, but on the other side of us. The problem is that it's a Dog one. We're in imperial territory."

Even Nhi, who wasn't very good at politics, could see the issue of bringing back a Dog corpse to a Dog Needle. "Still—"

"We'll lose face," Hạc Cúc said. "Not just us, personally. The clans. There are whispers already throughout the empire that the clans are greedy. That we take people's hard-earned money so the common people can travel through space safely and hoard it. If we can't find a tangler, and the only thing we have to show for ourselves is a dead imperial official . . ."

"It's the right thing to do."

"According to *you*. That's not part of my code." Soft laughter again, that look that weighed Nhi, as if deciding whether to ram her through. Nhi had said the wrong thing again, or perhaps there was no right thing to be said.

"Your code does include catching tanglers, doesn't it?"

"And?"

"Our best chance is if we have the resources."

"I agree with the sentiment, but being tied down by politics isn't resources. It's a waste of time. Let's report the death to the militia, and have it work its way upwards through the proper channels. It'll give us a few more days."

"To solve a murder and catch a tangler?"

A smile, from Hạc Cúc. "Why not?" And, more seriously: "I hear your fears. We can still send a message to the Dog Needle. Just not right away. Anyway, they're Dogs. You saw Ly Châu. They're incompetent. They're a lesser clan, only here to keep an eye on what we're doing. Their navigator capacities are bad. Or else why would they become imperials?"

Because they wanted safety. Because they didn't want to be beholden to the clans. Because the clan's rules and justice—each clan had its own, and each clan was sovereign in its own space, though the Council of the Eight Elders made sure some rules were absolute—made no sense to them. Nhi ran through all of those things in her head, and didn't say them. But she did know that they were in trouble, and there was little sense in adding more trouble. "Don't you have contact with your sư phụ? Through other means?"

A searching look, from Hạc Cúc. "Yes."

Nhi knew the value of a secret when it was given to her. "Thank you."

"For what?"

"The confidences."

Another of those searching looks that held her in utter stillness. "I assume you won't use that against me."

"No," Nhi said, with a confidence she didn't feel. She didn't pass on secrets or betray them, but it seemed to drive people away nevertheless.

"Can you—"

"Send him a message? I can," Hạc Cúc said. "It'll be faster, but it'll still take a few days before he can sort things out for us."

Which meant they needed to sort this out first. No easy way out of here. "Be that as it may."

Another searching and piercing look from Hạc Cúc. "I guess you're in charge, then. Chị." A pronoun reserved for a slightly elder peer—not the impersonal ones they'd been using with each other.

"*We,*" Nhi said.

Soft laughter from Hạc Cúc. She held out her hand again; this time Nhi took it, and held it for a moment, feeling the worn, unfamiliar weight of it in her own. "So be it. For better or for worse. We." Nhi had used a pronoun that encompassed all four juniors, but the one Hạc Cúc used was just the two of them, and Nhi felt a shiver run down her spine at that. A slight thrill, as if she were the one flirting with danger and unsure of what it all meant.

2

THE OLD RISE

Nhi had expected the mission to be a disaster, but not to turn sour so fast. Bảo Duy, the Rat junior, was about the only person who wasn't an issue: she was driven by curiosity and a thirst for danger and experimentations Nhi had seldom seen in Rats—who liked experiments but tended to be homebodies. A quick search on the network had established facts that weren't really secrets about her: she had a tendency to dangerous experiments involving tanglers and the Hollows, and a gift for talking other people into them. Long story short, the Rat clan must have felt a pressing need to send Bảo Duy somewhere where the only life she could endanger was her own.

No, the issue was everyone else. With Ly Châu's death, they were trying to deal with each other—and it was barely working. Lành was even more bitter and angry than usual, and Hạc Cúc's needling was making it worse.

Hạc Cúc.

Nhi hadn't expected Hạc Cúc. She hadn't expected to *resonate* with Hạc Cúc so much. It was an odd and unexpected feeling, and she'd left their meeting feeling oddly energised—and wondering what it would be like if they saw more of each other.

No.

No. That wasn't a good idea. She knew what happened every single time she tried this. She'd do or say something that was wrong—tell too much truth, drag too many secrets into the light, dealing blows to her girlfriend without meaning to. And people would leave, as they always did—and Nhi would go back to her archives and her secrets and her despondent acceptance that truth tellers, secret holders would always be alone. That love happened to other people. Not her.

It wasn't worth it. She'd had enough pain, and she could spare herself that one.

She forced herself to focus on what Bảo Duy was saying. "The fight she got in was with a tangler, but it wasn't here."

"Why the tendrils?" Hạc Cúc asked. They'd retreated to the juniors' room, where Bảo Duy had reconfigured the window-screen to display the entirety of the Silver Stream. A little arrow pointed to their own location.

Bảo Duy said, "It got snapped off, I think."

"*That* can happen?" Hạc Cúc was kneeling by the window-screen, long sleeves displaying the token of the Snake clan on the fabric. There was nothing submissive whatsoever about this gesture.

"Of course it can," Lành said. She sounded annoyed again, like that time she and Nhi had been sent to track down some contraband tea and found a whole network of illicit warehouses on three different planets. The paperwork mess had been epic.

Hạc Cúc threw Lành a glance, but didn't say anything.

Nhi released the breath she'd been holding. "Let's assume I've had my share of finding out weird things. Explain. How and why?"

Bảo Duy picked a candied lotus seed from the array on the table. "If you fight a tangler—which is a terrible idea—then it can lose a bit of a tendril. And you can drag it with you. It fades."

"Because it gets inside your body," Lành said. She sounded bleak. Lived experience, no doubt. Nhi had read the incident report, and asked other people: Lành had multiple scars from those years, the marks of tendrils that had wrapped themselves around her during the ship's crash.

"Fight a tangler. That means she found it. And then just crawled back to the inn to die?"

"I don't understand how she fought the tangler," Hạc Cúc said. "Did she use her Shadow?"

Bảo Duy shook her head. "On a *shuttle*? It wouldn't have been able to bear a prolonged fight with Shadow." A little use of Shadow was just going to cause minor damage to a shuttle, but any prolonged use on something that flimsy was going to cause things to leak out, starting with heat and oxygen. The clan ships were reinforced to avoid this.

"Then not on a ship, just on herself. Like a duel between navigators playing out planetside," Hạc Cúc said. And then stopped. "No, tanglers are too large."

"Also," Nhi said, drily, "I assume tanglers don't poison people with Nebula Cinnabar. Did you find anything about that?"

"She came back late," Lành said. "She received no guests in her room."

"How certain are we of this?" Nhi asked.

"The owner monitors oxygen rates and temperature," Lành said. "So fairly certain, unless said guest didn't breathe and had no heat signature."

Hạc Cúc said, "If the owner does this, they know when she died."

"Yes. Bi-hour of the Tiger, second eighth, more or less. Is that helpful?"

"No," Lành said.

"She was poisoned outside," Hạc Cúc said. "By the time she came back, she was already dying. What I don't understand is where she was poisoned."

Nhi said the obvious, "Nebula Cinnabar is a clan poison. Anyone here on clan business?"

"Us," Bảo Duy said, drily. Nhi felt a wave of affection for the Rat; it was a tense situation, and she could still summon non-wounding sarcasm, which took guts.

"Aside from us," Lành snapped. "We've already established we didn't do it."

"Let's just say we've agreed to trust each other," Hạc Cúc said. She stared at the map of the Silver Stream. "You said she came back late. When did she leave?"

"Bi-hour of the Pig, third eighth, tenth moment," Lành said.

Hạc Cúc drew a long, thin line from where they were to a point on the map that meant nothing to Nhi. "Here," she said. "Time to go there, stay perhaps half a bi-hour, and then leave."

"What's there?"

Hạc Cúc's face was grim. "It's a place called the Old Rise. A large cluster of buildings that failed."

"Failed?"

"No oxygen anymore. Just ruins. And some dead bodies, maybe. The vacuum would keep them more or less preserved."

Lành made a face. "You're going to need to explain to me why that place."

"Because that's where people have been going missing," Hạc Cúc said.

"Tangler's hideout?" Nhi asked.

"Maybe." Hạc Cúc's face was hard. "Or just a fight with smugglers, or clan people who didn't agree with who she was."

The juniors stared at each other somberly. Nhi could read that particular mood easily: clan people meant some of their own, and no one wanted to get into that kind of mess.

This is a terrible idea," Lành said. She was fiddling with her Shadow; it kept appearing and disappearing, trembling on the shuttle's walls. "Shouldn't we take a clan ship?"

"We don't have a clan ship," Bảo Duy said, sharply.

"Well, if we had a clan ship, we would definitely not have to put up with your piloting!" Lành said, clinging to the bench.

The shuttle was swerving wildly as Bảo Duy was fiddling with the controls; she'd manifested her Shadow to "help" with her effusive and fast Hairpin Ripples style—which mostly meant that every single alarm was blaring as they moved through the Fragments, not just the proximity ones.

"At least don't summon your Shadow. We're not going to be left with anything to breathe!"

"Would you rather we hit a rock?"

"I'd rather we got someone else to drive!" Lành's knuckles were white. "I can't believe your clan would let you pilot anything!"

Bảo Duy's voice was freezing. "There is absolutely nothing wrong with my piloting."

"I don't even understand how they let you open navigation gates. It's meant to require quiet and isolation, not weaving around like a rabbit on too much tea!"

A snort from Bảo Duy. "My gates are *fine*. And you know we're not opening a gate here."

"No, of course we're not. We'll just get *dragged* into it! That's what happens when you don't have a clan ship to protect yourself—"

Hạc Cúc was trying to ignore them. She was on her comms device, isolating herself at the back of the shuttle they'd hired to go to the Old Rise while Lành and Bảo Duy bickered over the commands. The shuttle was a small thing: a control deck at the front, two long benches going from the deck to the back, and a small hold belowdecks where Bảo Duy and Nhi had stored various supplies that they'd taken from Lý Châu's rooms. It was much, much smaller than Hạc Cúc's *The Steel Clam*—which, contrary to what she'd said, she did have nearby. She probably was the only one of the juniors who had her own ship, and there was absolutely no way she was letting Bảo Duy or anyone else anywhere near the controls.

Việt Nhi was sleeping on the leftmost bench, nearby, her head just a forearm's length from where Hạc Cúc was sitting. Hạc Cúc was impressed. It took some gumption to be able to totally ignore Bảo Duy's wild piloting.

Hạc Cúc put up a privacy screen and took the message from her sư phụ.

"Hạc Cúc," Sư phụ Quang Lộc said. He was looking more fragile than she remembered, his small beard streaked with white, his bald head gleaming in some invisible light. "The Eight Elders are investigating the crash." He sounded worried, too. "There's evidence it was deliberate."

Deliberate. "Ninth Judge?" she said, aloud. She'd summoned just enough of her own Shadow—the Divine Harmony she and Quang Lộc practiced enabled them to communicate by projecting her Shadow to the nearest Needle. In the rush of Bảo Duy's Shadow, Hạc Cúc's use of her own powers would go unnoticed. But they wouldn't have much time: the Old Rise wasn't that far.

"Ninth Judge was a skilled navigator. And a careful one."

"You think—"

Quang Lộc's voice was dark. "I think the empire has been trying to push us out for a while. They don't enjoy that we provide fast space travel. They'd rather it was all done by the Dogs."

"The Dogs don't have the talent." Hạc Cúc thought of Ly Châu, bossing everyone around and treating everyone with contempt, but incapable of making any progress on finding the tangler. Had it all been an act?

She'd died of Nebula Cinnabar poisoning. Of that, Hạc Cúc was sure. There'd been some impairment due to the tangler's sting, but not enough to kill her. But how in Heaven had she managed to go somewhere to find a tangler, and yet not drag the juniors—the ones she'd been incessantly driving to do the dirty and menial tasks—to face it?

"The Dogs don't have the talent," Quang Lộc said. "But they don't need to. If there was a big enough accident on our watch, if the tangler wasn't caught. If it went to a major population center and caused a disaster . . ."

Then, yes, of course, people would turn against the four

major navigator clans—the ones unable to protect them. Especially if the empire had spoken enough about the greed of the navigators. Never mind that ships and Needles and spaceports were expensive. Hạc Cúc shivered. "Yes. I see that."

"You see why it's imperative you succeed."

"Here's something I don't understand," Hạc Cúc said. She looked at where Lành was still arguing with Bảo Duy, who was now aglow with Shadow. The shuttle was spinning—Hạc Cúc extended her magnetic clamps and unthinkingly grabbed Nhi, dragging her into her lap and holding her there as the ship spun. Nhi didn't even stir. "Bảo Duy was all but kicked out of her clan after that experiment with the two tanglers at the Rat's fortress. Lành is an orphan with no connection and unpredictable powers. Nhi is an ineffective book nerd and an introvert with none of the aggressiveness of the Roosters. And I—" She wanted to say the words. To say that she was a failure. That she'd never live up to her own sư phụ's reputation. That she couldn't be as good, as kind as Quang Lộc was. But she couldn't. If she spoke them, she'd make them real. She'd have to watch Quang Lộc's face as he realized it, too.

"You're my apprentice," Quang Lộc said, simply. "And my heir. That matters more than you believe it does."

That was only because Quang Lộc didn't really see who Hạc Cúc really was. Hạc Cúc said, slowly, "What I don't understand is this: catching a tangler and sending it back to the Hollows is dangerous business. We own exactly one ship between the four of us. We're—" They were the very definition of expendable. Why send them on something this important?

A sigh, from Quang Lộc.

"Was this meant to leave the empire to look good when they swooped in? Because that's not going to work. Ly Châu is dead."

"So you told me. I don't know. I'll make enquiries. But it is odd."

Hạc Cúc folded her Shadow—and looked down to see Nhi had her eyes open, and was staring straight at her. Of course, she should have known. It wasn't just Snakes that could be sneaky. Little devil. "How long have you been listening?"

A shrug, from Nhi. "Long enough." She didn't move from Hạc Cúc's lap. "It is rather comfortable."

"You're not going to find it comfortable if I kill you," Hạc Cúc snapped.

"Oh?" A raised eyebrow from Nhi. "I'll look forward to your explaining to the elders why five of us left, and only three of us came back."

"You'll be dead!"

"But my ghost will possibly be *very* entertained," Nhi said. And winked at her, a horrible expression that would have made Hạc Cúc lose her temper further, if she had any temper left to be lost. A more serious look. "You know I don't share secrets lightly."

"Not even with your elders?"

Another shrug. "I don't like my elders particularly."

Hạc Cúc, staring into those mesmerising eyes—feeling the weight of Nhi in her lap, the utter, unwise vulnerability of her, lying in a Snake's lap with no defenses—asked a reckless question. "Then who is it that you like?"

A look, from Nhi—another of those searching ones that felt like Hạc Cúc was being dissected. "Not many people, really. But you knew that." An amused laugh. "An ineffective book nerd."

Too late, Hạc Cúc remembered that the conversation with Quang Lộc had included her rather brutal assessment of everyone in the shuttle. "I'm sorry," she said.

"Don't be," Nhi said. "I say far unkinder things about myself. But I'm curious."

In spite of herself, Hạc Cúc found herself bending closer to Nhi. "About what?"

A smile from Nhi—an expression that utterly transformed her round, moon-shaped face. "You stopped before saying anything about yourself. What is it you were going to say?"

Flawed. Failure. Forever unable to live up to her sư phụ's reputation. Unloved. All these went through Hạc Cúc's mind, a heartbeat before she snapped, "None of your business."

Nhi unfolded herself, bowed to her. The gesture was sarcastic. What she said next wasn't. "Fair. I hope one day you can bring yourself to say it." There was no irony in her voice, just utter seriousness.

Hạc Cúc stared into Nhi's eyes. Her gaze held her and she couldn't look away; there was an odd, flushed heat in her chest that wasn't her Shadow. "What?"

Nhi shook her head. "If you don't want to say it, I'm not going to say it for you." She kept one hand on the shuttle's metal walls, the magnetic clamp holding her in place.

Hạc Cúc fell back on the familiar. She pointed to Lành, who was still arguing vociferously with Bảo Duy. "I think we should stop the bickering. And the reckless piloting. If it's smugglers in the Old Rise, we should probably make a more inconspicuous arrival."

Nhi laughed. "How's your piloting?"

Hạc Cúc couldn't help but laugh. "Terrible," she said. "But it gets people places and it doesn't get me noticed if I don't need to be." She'd parked *The Steel Clam* near one of the larger Fragments; she wanted to be sure she could leave if she needed to, even if leaving required rallying the Dog Needle and charming them into letting her pass. And she could take Nhi, too.

No.

No.

That was a terrible idea. As soon as Nhi realized who she was—that there was nothing of care, nothing of what had made her sư phụ great and beloved in the void and stars circles—she'd leave.

Something screeched, and the shuttle slowed to a dead stop—the inertia jostling Hạc Cúc. She sighed. "I think we should do something about the driving."

Nhi broke off eye contact and said, "Thank you for all the information on everyone else." She winked. "I'll be back." She walked to Lành, who was still trying to convince Bảo Duy to slow down.

Lành looked up. Nhi said, "This is a den of smugglers. I'm going to need someone else to pilot if we want to not be unduly noticed as we arrive."

Bảo Duy weighed Nhi up for a while. "Makes sense," she said, and stepped away from the controls, folding her Shadow back. The alarms finally fell silent; Hạc Cúc hadn't realized how annoying they were until they stopped. "Have at them," she said.

"Good," Lành said, drawling. "Finally some competence."

Nhi said nothing. She changed the shuttle's front-window display to show the front and sides of the shuttle, and piloted the same way she wielded Shadow—slow and ponderous, the various Fragments filling the display and then remaining on it. It should have been laborious, but it was oddly graceful; rock debris of the Silver Stream came at them in clumps and clouds, moved their way by the vagaries of gravity, and through it all Nhi made only minute adjustments to the trajectory of the shuttle. It was as if she was anticipating whatever the Silver Stream was throwing at them well in advance of when it would show up—weaving a mesmerising pattern of her own between the smaller Fragments.

This close to the Old Rise, there were no clusters of buildings, only, from time to time, the pings of rescue beacons on the odd smaller Fragment, a steady light that entered the window and then left.

"Here," Hạc Cúc said.

It was a much larger Fragment, where buildings clung to the sides of huge canyons that were too deep and too dark for her to see the bottom of. They poked at all angles, unconstrained by gravity.

"No sign of life," Bảo Duy said, frowning. She had her Shadow around her, drawn for defense. The pressure of it was making the walls of the shuttle tremble; it was no reinforced clan ship, and it was going to lose oxygen if Bảo Duy didn't fold her Shadow back into herself. Hạc Cúc braced herself for the alarms to blare again, and decided she didn't have to put up with any of that.

"Stop with the Shadow," she said, walking closer to Bảo Duy and looming over her. "Or it'll get extremely unpleasant."

Nhi didn't even look up from the controls. "Please stop threatening people. It's about as effective as using chopsticks to stab them."

How could she go from those fragile moments of understanding to being this utterly annoying? "Oh, believe me, I can stab you with chopsticks," Hạc Cúc snapped. "In your sleep."

Nhi smiled. "I'll have that to look forward to, then, won't I?" She nosed the shuttle towards a large gap in the canyon walls—as they got closer, Hạc Cúc saw the glint of broken approach beacons. Smuggler territory all right: there was no life or even basic safety measures. The perfect place to run some merchandise someone didn't want the empire or the clans to know about.

"All right," Nhi said after the shuttle had landed. "The suits and gliders are in the back. We also have barrier generators, just in case." Barrier generators were for creating a large bubble around a tangler that would trap it. At which point more experienced people in the clans would usually take over and kill the tangler.

They didn't have more experienced people from the clans, and somehow Hạc Cúc wasn't convinced that they could even put the barrier generators to good use. But so far, what Nhi was suggesting was just looking around, which was a very different—and hopefully easier—prospect.

"Good," Hạc Cúc said, shortly.

Nhi said, "Let's go see who's around." She turned to Lành, who'd been strangely silent the entire time. Cowed into submission? That seemed extremely unlike her.

"Was anything the matter?" Lành asked.

Nhi said, "We're going to need someone to stay with the shuttle to be sure no one makes away with it. Why don't you?"

Lành stared at Nhi for a while. "You're mistaken," she said, coldly. "This shuttle has bio-coded clamps. We can leave it here, keyed to our ID, and no one will be able to make away with it."

"Mistaken. Am I?" Nhi held her gaze for a while. "The offer stands," she said, coolly and calmly. "I still think it would be better to have someone here."

Hạc Cúc caught up with Nhi as they exited the shuttle—the other two were ahead, floating under the wall of the cavern. "What was that about?"

A weighing gaze, from Nhi. "You know."

"No. I don't. I don't see why you'd needlessly antagonize Lành. That's my job. And why would she be so angry at you?"

Nhi said, softly, "We're going to find a tangler. A creature that likely harmed Ly Châu, possibly made her vulnerable to poison."

"And why would—" Hạc Cúc stopped then. "Oh. You think Lành is scared."

"I know Lành is scared," Nhi said. She made a weird, deprecating, and oddly vulnerable gesture with her shoulders that suddenly made Hạc Cúc feel warmth under her collarbone. "First, because I've worked with her. And second, because I'm very familiar with how cutting one can be, when one wants to mask fear."

"From your own experience?" Hạc Cúc stared at her.

Soft laughter from Nhi. Hạc Cúc suddenly had this odd,

almost prescient intuition that she was going to deflect. She grabbed Nhi's hand, barely feeling it through layers of suit. "Don't," she said.

"Don't do what?"

"Don't joke and use sarcasm to get out of the truth."

Nhi stopped, as if she'd been shocked by a jolt of energy. "The truth," she said, as if chewing on it. "Fine. No, I don't do that when I'm scared. But I do it when I want to be alone."

"Does that happen often?"

A sigh, from Nhi. "Most of the time." She gestured towards the rock cave. "Shall we?"

Hạc Cúc watched her drift away and then engage her glider once she was well clear of the shuttle. The warmth under her collarbone had spread to her chest and cheeks; she felt she was burning from something that wasn't embarrassment or anger, but that same odd feeling of connection she'd felt before, that hint of deeper possibilities.

She was twenty-five, and was not lacking life experience or common sense altogether. The string of relationships she'd had was long; those relationships that had been meaningful far shorter. Her longest relationship had been Linh—another Snake, drawn by the aura of the Pure Heart Master—who had left when she'd realized, as Hạc Cúc already knew deep in her bones, that Hạc Cúc would never be half the person her sư phụ was.

Maybe she should have a fling with Nhi. Sleep with her, get it out of their systems. But no, that would be unkind and unfair to Nhi, and if there was one thing that Hạc Cúc could do, it was follow her code.

No. They were going to keep this—whatever this odd,

growing dance of connections and irritations—friends only. They were going to find a tangler, get rid of whatever problems this mission really was bringing, and then she was going to go home, and train with her sư phụ again, to try—and fail—to live up to the potential Quang Lộc had seen in her.

She could do this. She could keep it all under control.

3

STROBILATION

Nhi knew this mission was going to be trouble, and Hạc Cúc made it even worse. She was by turns acid and infuriating, and by turns oddly vulnerable and straightforward in a way that made Nhi want to touch her—and Heaven knew Nhi wasn't the kind of person who touched others. Touch was always fraught for Nhi, something that everyone found natural but that, to her, felt like too much, a breaking of some unspoken rule or law. Nhi could feel the tension in the air between them, and it wasn't helping one bit.

As to the others . . . Bảo Duy was endearing but reckless, and Lành was extremely difficult to deal with or protect, which added to the annoyance.

The gliders were small, and they were flat, about the size of Nhi's torso, and shaped like a large triangle with a blunt, flattish head. There were two magnetic holds that connected to clamps they had in their suits. Each glider had a small motor, powerful enough to move one person at perhaps half the speed of the shuttle, and their suits kept them from dying in the vacuum. A glider wasn't as powerful or as maneuverable as a shuttle, and even less than a ship in the hands of a skilled navigator and their Shadow—but for what they had to do, it would serve.

As they moved down the canyon, they all drew Shadow to them, shimmering veils that manifested differently for each of them: Hạc Cúc's Divine Harmony was aggressive but discreet, Bảo Duy's Hairpin Ripples exuberant and fast, and Lành's Ambush in the Grass dark and quiet. Nhi could see why Lành was isolated among her own clan; her Shadow was dark, pulsing through with light patterns that were reminiscent of tanglers, and even the way she moved clinging to her glider—oddly jerky, with pulses shooting through her Shadow—didn't really seem to belong to the Ox clan. Or to any clan.

Nhi herself wasn't really fazed; people were weird, and who was she to judge? Plus, they were trying to deal with a tangler. And smugglers who presumably would be none too happy to see them. She scanned the canyon's walls: nothing. Just abandoned buildings with windows that weren't sealed anymore, and stark gloom over shuttles that were a little too still and cold to still be in possession of a functional life-support system. No movement. No tendrils. Not that she could see. The tendrils were the worst, because they were so much longer than the tangler's body, and they didn't actually exist in the physical world, so they could cut through walls, or shuttles, or rock. Shadow would stop them, if wielded by someone who'd received the appropriate training. Which hopefully was the case with everyone on this mission.

Nhi's veils of Shadow bumped against the canyon's walls. Still nothing but the faint pressure of rock. Darkness—the canyon seemed bottomless. The sound of her own breath.

"Wait," Hạc Cúc said, over the comms. "There's something—"

Nhi drew her Shadow closer, ready to strike. She felt it build up in her belly near the vitality center, just as Hạc Cúc angled her glider towards one of the openings in the canyon's walls, one below them that was almost hidden by the gloom. "Chị, don't—" Nhi said, a ball of fear building in her innards.

The comms went silent. Lành was cautiously circling. "There's no tangler," she said, firmly.

"You sound very certain," Bảo Duy said.

"That's what I get for being left alone in the dark with them," Lành said. "I can sense them."

"And talk to them?" Bảo Duy asked.

A snort from Lành. "They don't really talk," she said.

"But—"

"Can't you take a hint?" Lành snapped. "I'm not talking about this further."

Nhi hadn't known any of this about Lành: it was a surprise. She filed it in her brain alongside the other things she knew about her. Maybe it'd help her deal with Lành. For some reason, it was harder to this time around. Too many new variables, too many new behaviors Nhi couldn't predict.

Where was Hạc Cúc? Nhi scanned the darkness. "Chị, come back."

A soft ping on her comms. "You'd better come down, em." Hạc Cúc's voice was bleak. "Just very, very quietly, will you? And very carefully. I'll guide you."

"Have you found the tangler?" Bảo Duy asked.

Nhi's ears prickled. She'd have said so, if she had. So it was something else. "That'd be too easy, wouldn't it?"

"I'll send you a trajectory," Hạc Cúc said.

It was mostly a straight curve, but as Nhi set the glider to follow it—as she descended into darkness, and the mouth of the opening in the canyon wall loomed over her—she saw that it ended with a strong braking, and that the entire space beyond its ending was blotted out as forbidden. So, caution. Very strong caution.

She drew her Shadow closer, and that's when she felt the first bumps against it. Soft and barely perceptible. "Chị—" she said to Hạc Cúc, on a private channel.

"I know," Hạc Cúc said. "Just come here."

The opening was the beginning of a cave that flared into a larger corridor, heading off into darkness.

Inside, Hạc Cúc was floating vertically by the side of two corpses. They had to be corpses, because they didn't move, and they also didn't give off any heat on the sensors. She'd clamped them to one of the cave's walls and had turned off the motor of her glider, which she was clinging to by one hand. Nhi couldn't see the corpses' faces, but the network of long, thin slashes across the suits was obvious. Tendrils. A lot of tendrils, the same ones she could feel bumping against her defenses. Too far away yet to do much damage, but if the umbrella—the main body—of the tangler moved . . . She fought back a sense of rising panic. She couldn't afford it. They couldn't afford it.

"Smugglers?" she asked, to Hạc Cúc.

Hạc Cúc wasn't answering. She was watching the darkness, carefully. Nhi moved, feeling the pressure of the tendrils increase against her Shadow. Oh, this was bad. Really bad. "How far is the umbrella?"

"That's the problem," Hạc Cúc said.

Bảo Duy pushed past them, Shadow unfolding into the

tunnel. She was softly cursing, words that would have had the elders of Nhi's clan discipline her.

"They died of being stung," Lành said, behind them. "But there's no tangler—"

"Tendrils," Nhi said, sharply. "The tunnel is full of tendrils."

"There's no umbrella," Bảo Duy said, sharply.

"What do you mean, there's no umbrella?"

"Watch, because I won't do it twice," Hạc Cúc said. She did something with her free hand, and her Shadow left her, flowing towards the tunnel. It outlined everything, except the thin shapes of tendrils, which showed up as lighter shapes that couldn't be touched by Shadow. In the split moment—less than a breath—that it lit up everything, she saw what Hạc Cúc meant: it wasn't the trailing mass she'd expected, but instead a dense surface across the tunnel, like a fishing net. The tendrils were sprouting from the walls themselves.

That was *wrong*.

A sharp intake of breath, from Bảo Duy. "Strobilation."

"That's impossible," Lành said. "You've got it wrong."

"I never get it wrong," Bảo Duy said.

All right, that wasn't just wrong. It was bad, bad news.

Nhi said it out loud, in a less technical fashion. "It's blooming, isn't it?"

"That's why we can't see the bigger tendrils," Bảo Duy said. "Tanglers tend to reabsorb them when they bloom."

A bloom was a pullulation. A phenomenon most navigators knew to flee from. Sometimes tanglers would just . . . fruit. Drop seeds that split and split into multiple smaller tanglers. That was a strobilation: a scattering of seeds. But no tangler had ever done it outside of the Hollows.

"We need to warn someone," Nhi said.

"No. We need to kill that large one first." Bảo Duy's voice was sharp, which was in and of itself worrying, because the Rat navigator had been soft-spoken so far. It made Nhi nervous. All right, more nervous than she currently was, with the tendrils pressing against her Shadow. No wonder there were no smugglers, if the tunnels nearby were full of tendrils. They were all dead, and it hadn't been a fast or painless death—they'd have convulsed, choking as their bodies forgot to move, to breathe.

"Why?" Nhi asked.

"Because so far, it's the only one that can bloom. The small ones won't be able to make more of themselves until they've grown."

"And that's going to take how much time?" Nhi asked.

"What I'm more interested in," Hạc Cúc said, sharply, "is how you know all this. Because no one's actually seen tanglers outside the Hollows."

"That's not quite true. You know there have been incidents before."

"You know what I mean," Hạc Cúc said, sharply.

"Is this really the best time to quarrel?" Nhi asked, more forcefully than she meant.

"No time like the present," Lành said. She sounded almost amused. People were just *weird*.

"All right, all right," Bảo Duy said. "You want me to say it? I know it because I've run experiments."

"Because you've killed people to find out about tanglers," Hạc Cúc said. She sounded angry.

"Because you don't kill people?"

"Only those who deserve it."

"They *volunteered*," Bảo Duy said, sharply.

"And that still doesn't make it right."

Nhi forced herself to take a deep breath. She had to do something, because if she didn't, Hạc Cúc was going to try to kill Bảo Duy for breaching Hạc Cúc's code—Nhi didn't know which part of her code, but she could certainly understand having rules that were sacred. But equally, they needed Bảo Duy's expertise, and they most certainly didn't need to add another corpse to that freaky cave. She needed to stop the argument and she only knew one way to stop an argument, but it was going to be really unpleasant.

Unpleasant was better than dead, though, and the pressure against her Shadow was increasing, which didn't bode well for their survival. "It's really nice to see that you're more effective at killing each other than tanglers, but also regrettable," she said, with her best drawl. Her arms were shaking with the pressure to hold the tendrils away. Tanglers this small weren't smart, but they'd have hunting instincts all the same. And it was stressful to not be able to see the tendrils. In the Hollows they'd have been visible, but this wasn't the Hollows.

"Who elected you leader of the party again?" Hạc Cúc asked.

"I wasn't planning on it," Nhi said, "but clearly the minimum criterion was bring everyone back alive. Which you're not doing at the moment."

Hạc Cúc moved away as if hurt. Chewing on a clever comeback, no doubt. Nhi tackled Bảo Duy next. "Two questions, Rat."

"I'm more than my clan," Bảo Duy snapped. Good, it was working.

"Can they move? And how long do we have?"

"They're *seeds*," Bảo Duy said. She still sounded annoyed, but at least it wasn't at Hạc Cúc. "They can't move."

"How long do we have?" Nhi realized, with a touch of annoyance at herself, that the question was ambiguous. "How long until they move? And how long until they can bloom?" Her hands were shaking; she could barely hold on to her glider. Being this close to tanglers was mentally exhausting. If they could move, they'd have done it surely? But that's what the smugglers might have thought, until the first lash of a tendril went through their suit . . .

"They're turning towards us." Bảo Duy's voice was emotionless. Lành, who hadn't said much, moved away from the corpses and towards the opening of the cave. Nhi couldn't blame her. She could feel Hạc Cúc tensing, ready to lash out at someone, anyone. And it was going to be Lành, and it was going to be a disaster if she did. She spoke up before it could happen.

"And? That doesn't answer either question."

"No, but it did seem the most pressing concern," Bảo Duy said. "A few days before they can move. And months before they can bloom."

All right, so the bloom wasn't the issue. Which was good, she guessed? For a definition of good that involved being in the same space as killer creatures with one of them making more. "And the large one?"

"If it's fed, it'll make more. That'll take bi-hours. Or possibly centidays. Seeing as there's eight centidays in a bi-hour . . ."

"Yes, yes," Hạc Cúc snapped. "Don't go all Rat at me, please. I don't need the technical details. I don't believe these were the only two smugglers on this rock," Hạc Cúc said. Her hands had moved; she was holding to the glider with one, and with the other she'd pulled out a large stun gun that Nhi was pretty sure wasn't standard issue with the suits in the rented shuttle. "So we can assume it fed a lot more, and it's making a lot more seeds."

"Can we do the sensible thing and be arguing *outside* of that cave, away from the killer creatures?" Lành asked. Wounding again: she was upset. Very upset.

Hạc Cúc cocked her head to stare at her over the glider's lights. "You have a point," she said, grudgingly. "Dear leader?" It was mocking. Nhi hadn't expected it to hurt quite so much; she was so used to people being angry or sarcastic at her. But somehow Hạc Cúc knew how to get under her skin.

She did the only sensible thing *she* could do, which was ignore it. "Let's go," she said.

Even with the gliders at full speed, it was nerve-rackingly slow. Lành was looking away from the cave, gaze resolutely fixed ahead and Shadow shimmering around her. Hạc Cúc was hanging on to her glider, watching the cave, with a gun trained on it. Bảo Duy was talking over the comms, the only one who seemed excited. Nhi . . . Nhi couldn't wait to be out of range. Why had the elders thought she was the best the person for the job?

"The main one has to be further on in the canyon. We can follow the trail of seeds—"

"Or corpses," Hạc Cúc said, bleakly.

At the shuttle, no one let go of their Shadow until they were sure that they were safe. Nhi held on to hers nevertheless; it was going to be exhausting, but she wanted to be prepared for the eventuality of tanglers coming their way.

"All right," she said, since they were all looking at her and it looked like no one was going to say anything. She wasn't even the eldest in the party—she was pretty sure that was Lành or Hạc Cúc. "Tell me again why we're not warning the elders and just letting them handle this."

"Because it's half a day to get back to the Silver Stream, two days to the nearest Needle, a lot of embarrassing explanations about why we have a dead Dog—I'm sure no one forgot Ly Châu, did they?—and then another few days until the elders can actually get here. And in the meantime, the big one is making more tanglers," Bảo Duy said. She was leaning on the wall, more alive and excited than Nhi had ever seen her.

Enthusiasm was good; what was less good was that Nhi wasn't quite sure Bảo Duy was very skilled at keeping herself—or others—alive. And Nhi had forgotten Ly Châu, which she was briefly ashamed of.

"*I* haven't forgotten Ly Châu," Hạc Cúc said in a tone that clearly suggested someone somewhere was going to pay for the murder. Or the inconvenience to Hạc Cúc, it wasn't clear. "But she's not the emergency right now."

Nhi couldn't help it. "She came here. Ly Châu. She saw . . . this." And then . . . then she'd gone back to the inn, except she'd died before it all came to a head.

A brief laugh from Hạc Cúc. "And then she decided to get some proper reinforcements instead of us? That tracks. Except the murderer found her first."

Lành said, "You're still advocating we face a tangler, something an imperial navigator walked away from?"

Nhi spoke before Hạc Cúc could, and before the situation with Lành degenerated even further. "Are you trying to suggest Dogs set some kind of standard for difficulty? Because we all know what they're worth. No one joins the empire's enforcers unless all the clans rejected them." It wasn't quite true. But it was what they all needed to hear.

There was a silence. Then laughter from Bảo Duy and Hạc Cúc, followed by a more reluctant laugh from Lành. "Dogs are so much hassle, eh?" Hạc Cúc said.

A collective sigh. Everyone had had to deal with Dogs, or imperial officials, at some point.

"There's still a murderer out there," Lành said, but it was more subdued. "They could be targeting us next."

"Us?" Hạc Cúc laughed. "We're really not worth it."

"But we're still going to kill a tangler?" Nhi asked. She'd looked it up before leaving. Most of the Rooster clan's techniques had to do with driving away tanglers, but there were obscure records that spoke of a more final end. "Do we know how to do that?"

Bảo Duy made a gesture with her hands. "Yes," she said. "I killed several, back at the Rat Fortress."

"But?" Nhi heard the doubt she wasn't voicing.

"But we've never tried it in those circumstances."

"When it's blooming?"

"When it's fed that much," Bảo Duy said. "It must be huge by now." There was something in her voice—not fear or distrust, but something of admiration.

"A little less worship of tanglers here," Lành snapped.

But of course Bảo Duy was fascinated by tanglers, and considering this a unique opportunity to study one in the matter world, regardless of the danger.

No, Bảo Duy definitely couldn't be trusted to keep herself alive.

"Will it be visible?" Hạc Cúc asked.

A shrug. "Yes. If you have eyes. If you have Shadow."

"That's not a yes," Nhi said, sharply.

"I can feel it," Lành said. She was shivering, and she sounded like she was about to throw up. "It's further on. In the canyon. It's . . . happy."

Happy. Nhi definitely didn't want to dwell too much on the implications of Lành knowing this.

Nhi called up a map from the energy-founts. "Where?" she asked, and Lành showed her.

"You have to trap it first," Bảo Duy said. She made a gesture, projecting from her personal comms terminal to the map-screen. "Here. You use the barrier generators to contain it. They'll key themselves to the tangler's tendrils, so they'll match its speed. At least for a little while."

"That's very imprecise," Nhi said.

Bảo Duy threw her hands up. "I thought you didn't want me to go all Rat on you. Fine, fine. The mean duration is a centiday. An eighth of a bi-hour for everyone who doesn't know."

Even children knew what a centiday stood for.

"Careful," Hạc Cúc said, warningly.

Nhi wrestled the conversation back on track. "The mean duration."

"Yes, it has a standard deviation of an eighth of a centiday. A fairly classical probability distribution, so outcomes beyond three standard deviations become rather improbable."

Hạc Cúc's gaze was intent. "So five-eighths of a centiday

as a worst possible case. That's the time we have to surround it with the barrier generators. Is it going to put up a fight?"

Bảo Duy's round face stretched into a grimace. "You want certainty. I don't have a distribution model for that. But it's never happened."

"That one is different," Lành said.

"Not that different," Bảo Duy said, finally. "I've seen this before. Just never at this scale. Trap it and kill it."

"Corner and then kill." Hạc Cúc sounded thoughtful. "That's more in my skill set."

"And you know how to kill one?" Lành asked, aggressively.

Hạc Cúc laughed. "We Snakes can kill anything. Or anyone." She not only still had her gun, she'd found a second one. And a knife with a polished blade that looked like the vacuum kind, sharp enough to cut through most materials. Leaning against the wall of the shuttle, with veils of Shadow shimmering around her, she looked like her clan's tutelary animal: coiled and ready to strike at a moment's notice—dangerously seductive, someone who'd be the death of Nhi rather than a lover.

Ughhhh. Nhi really didn't need those thoughts right now. Especially as Lành, angry and fearful, was on the offensive once again.

"Yes, of course," Lành said. Her voice was venomous. "You kill anyone and anything, for the right price. The morals you profess, which—"

"The morals you have not a shred of!"

It was going to get ugly again. Nhi moved, pushing herself effortlessly towards Hạc Cúc, and laid a hand on her wrist, just above where she was holding the gun. Hạc

Cúc's arm tensed, but she didn't throw Nhi off. Through her Shadow, Nhi felt Hạc Cúc—fast, aggressive, filled with coiled anger—pushing against her.

She'd put her hand on Hạc Cúc's body before, but this time felt different. This time . . . the tension wasn't only aggression.

"Morality won't save any of us," Nhi said, sharply.

A sharp look from Hạc Cúc. "And lack of morals might well doom us."

"Please don't kill Lành," Nhi said. "You can always kill each other after we deal with the tangler."

"Please?" A crinkle in Hạc Cúc's eyes, which might well have been a smile. "Are you begging me, em?" The affectionate diminutive—reserved for intimates—made Nhi feel weird inside, as if she was burning up, tangler-stung, and couldn't find words anymore.

"Yes. No. I mean."

Hạc Cúc's other hand moved to pluck Nhi's unresisting one from her wrist. Her gaze held Nhi's—not just held, but *doomed* Nhi, making that fire within her burn brighter and brighter, engulfing her whole. "For you, then, I suppose I can make an effort."

Nhi breathed, hard, fast. They were touching each other, hand to wrist, thin layers of flesh through Shadow, and it was unbearable to be so close, and yet it was everything she'd ever wanted.

She snatched her hand from Hạc Cúc's. "You're impossible," she said, but she didn't feel like she meant the reproach—"impossible" had turned into a wholly alien word, one that meant a marvel she hadn't anticipated and an irritation. "You're not making an effort for me. You're making an effort because we have a tangler. And as soon as we've taken a rest, we'll go retrieve the barrier generators and—"

Her brain caught up with her eyes. "Where's Bảo Duy?" she asked. It was just the three of them in the room.

And heard, softly, like the click of a gun, the sound of the airlock opening and closing.

"She's gone outside," Lành said.

Hạc Cúc caught up with Nhi on the way to the gliders. "She's left all the barrier generators in the holds. She's only got a glider and a suit."

"Do you know where she is?" Nhi said. She sounded disconsolate. Hạc Cúc fought the urge to hug her. The last time they'd touched had been . . . thrilling and discomfiting. She wasn't proud of herself, but flirting with Nhi had been like scratching an itch that wouldn't calm down. Except, of course, that just like scratching, it had done nothing to quench her growing feelings.

"I think it's a safe bet," Hạc Cúc said, "that Bảo Duy went to find the main tangler. She sounded far too excited about it. 'The first time any tangler has bloomed in an environment that's not the Hollows. It's such an opportunity to observe.'"

Nhi laughed, shortly. "You do sound like her."

"A little only. It'll be fine," Hạc Cúc said. She wasn't even sure why she said it. Because Nhi seemed so down, and it would have been mean to say what she really thought. Because Nhi was affecting her, because it was different to flirt with Nhi and to make her sad. Because she was soft, she supposed. Because being with Nhi—was weird but also strangely comforting. Like she didn't have to pretend to be who she wasn't. Like she didn't have to try to live up to false expectations.

"Do you believe that?" Nhi asked. "That it will all be fine?"

She could have lied, but it wouldn't have been fair. "For Bảo Duy? I don't know. But I believe we can still make a difference."

Nhi breathed out. She released the Shadow she'd been holding; Hạc Cúc felt its loss like a loss of light and life in the room. "How?" she asked.

If there was one thing life—and numerous missions—had taught Hạc Cúc, it was that nothing was ever truly lost, and that every plan needed fifteen different contingency ones. No one ever showed up for their own assassination according to plan. "Trap it," she said. "Fast. Badly, if need be. And then let's see what happens." She breathed out. "I'm going to get Lành."

"Don't," Nhi said. It was quiet, but it felt like the lash of a tangler's tendril.

"Why?"

"I'll get Lành," Nhi said.

Hạc Cúc stared at her. She wanted to make some joke, to say that Nhi was only doing that to make sure they all stayed alive, but Nhi was simply standing there, unmoving, with no trace of irony or sarcasm. The words shriveled in Hạc Cúc's throat. "Why?" she asked again.

A hesitation, from Nhi. Then she said, with a drawl, "Mostly so you two don't kill each other. It'd be a bad precedent." For a moment, she looked as though she was going to say something else, maybe ask another question—and

Hạc Cúc wasn't even sure of what she'd said. Before she could collect herself, Nhi had left the room.

Hạc Cúc stood there, with no one to get angry at but herself—which was a terrible way to handle anything.

She did it, anyway.

How did she keep putting herself in those situations? It felt like everything on this mission was fraught and unexpected. It felt . . . like being given things she didn't deserve and didn't know what to do with.

Usually she'd ask herself what Quang Lộc would do, but she was pretty sure her sư phụ had never had to deal with so much pent-up sexual frustration on top of the usual frustration of being stuck with juniors she despised at best, and actively hated at worst.

All right, she could do this. Control this, or at any rate make sure it didn't crash and burn. That *she* didn't crash and burn.

4

BARRIERS

They set off from the shuttle in subdued silence, their gliders heavy with weaponry, Shadow tightly wrapped around themselves.

They were dragging the barrier generators behind them; each of them was the size of a small energy-fount, large enough to be held in both hands. Lành had taken one look at them and reeled off a full list of technical specifications at a high clip, before Nhi put a hand on her shoulder and took her to a corner to sit down. Hạc Cúc had forced herself not to intervene, despite her itch to cut Lành to size. Knowing the full list of specifications was typically Lành—never waste an occasion to look good—but she'd fail them on some level before the mission was through. Missions required courage to stand up, and Lành didn't have that. There would be someone or something, some representative of authority she'd end up toadying to. Even if she didn't fold before, during the tangler's capture. No, Hạc Cúc would do the sensible thing, and consider Lành an asset that was unreliable at best, and actively malicious at worst. She genuinely couldn't understand what her sư phụ had seen in Lành. Saving her was one thing, but insisting Lành was worthy of him, and teaching her? How could he?

Hạc Cúc had activated the magnetic clamps on her

wrists to secure her position on the glider, and drawn her weapons. She was trying to remember everything about the Hollows she could, but most of the experience of a navigator was swathes of Shadow, odd lights, and a strange and tense feeling that nothing was quite making sense. She'd been lucky enough to only run into a tangler once, and it had been enough of an experience that she didn't feel like repeating it. Hạc Cúc liked being the hunter, but much less being the one hunted.

Nhi was sticking close to Hạc Cúc, her Shadow—Heavenly Weave—was slow and ponderous, gently brushing against Hạc Cúc's from time to time. It almost felt like they were standing side by side in spite of the layers of suits. It was . . . soothing. Everything she couldn't allow herself.

Lành was lagging behind, her own string of barrier generators slowly and lazily changing directions behind her because of her low speed. She had come along for appearance's sake. Or because Nhi could be strangely persuasive when she talked to people—her face aglow with an odd intensity that made Hạc Cúc's heart feel ten thousand sizes too big for her chest.

Hạc Cúc forced herself to focus on the tangler. At least that bit was predictable. She had asked Quang Lộc about killing a tangler, and her sư phụ had sounded thoughtful as he'd explained an ancestral clan technique, the Rain Cleaving Sharpness: a careful manipulation of Shadow that was meant to cut into a tangler's body.

Hạc Cúc had tried it in the cave, and it had worked, but it had drained her and made her more irritable than usual. And this had been a couple of small tanglers, still clinging to the walls. She couldn't even imagine what it would take to down a larger one.

Maybe, just maybe, she couldn't quite blame Lành for being so scared.

"I've pinged Bảo Duy," Nhi said. "Nothing. She's cut off her comms, I think."

Of course. Didn't want anyone to interfere with whatever scatterbrained plan she'd come up with. Something to see the tangler up close: the same kind of experiment she specialized in, the kind that ended in disaster. Though at least she hadn't talked anyone into it yet. Small mercies.

The walls of the canyon widened. Hạc Cúc kept her Shadow tightly around her, bracing herself for the slight push of tanglers against it. There was nothing. Not yet.

"Over there," Nhi said. Her Shadow, slow and ponderous, pushed against something, a pattern that made no sense. Bits and pieces. Where was the tangler? It was just darkness spread all around them: walls of sharp rocks on either side, with broken habitats still clinging to them—the occasional spur of rock with the cracked remains of a landing pad.

Wait.

It was a tangler. Just.

"It's *massive*," Hạc Cúc said, forcing herself to breathe.

It was bits and pieces, waving in some invisible current, visible as Nhi's Shadow pushed against them and then moving out of sight the next moment, the very tail end of tendrils with stingers, moving in the same direction at them but with a more erratic speed.

"Most of the tanglers I've seen have been smaller," Hạc

Cúc said. Much, much smaller. Human-sized, and even at that size the amount of damage they did to humans was incalculable.

"It's *huge*," Lành said. Her voice was fearful. "Almost as large as this canyon."

Which was six measures. A thousand-and-a-half times Hạc Cúc's size. "I'm not sure we can kill that," Hạc Cúc said.

"That's cute," Nhi said—she was in the lead again, flying in that same slow and ponderous pattern that somehow always avoided being too close to any of the stingers. "But not the priority."

Hạc Cúc saw red. "Really? We have a tangler that's growing and too large to stop, and that's not your priority? I thought you were smarter."

"Oh, I'm not that smart." Nhi didn't even sound fazed. "Two things, though. One: stopping doesn't mean killing, O Snake."

"I know that," Hạc Cúc snapped. What in Heaven did Nhi hope to achieve by annoying her? "And what's two?"

"Where is Bảo Duy?" Nhi asked, simply.

"She—" Hạc Cúc stopped. The glider's sensors weren't showing anything. "She's not here."

"She was." Nhi's voice was sharp. "Just a moment ago."

"She has to be here." Hạc Cúc pushed her glider a little further than Nhi—and felt the first bump of tendrils against her Shadow, the same feeling she'd had in the cave—something large and heavy and viscous, a touch that pressed and pressed further inwards, eating away at her Shadow.

"The tangler has her." Lành's voice was bleak.

"I'm the first to complain about undue optimism," Nhi said, "but this is really not the time to think of the worst."

Yes, because the worst was all of them dead in horrible circumstances. Hạc Cúc snorted. "Dear leader—" she started, and then realized that Nhi was doing the exact thing she'd said she'd do: being horribly unpleasant to push people away in the hopes they'd leave her alone.

But they couldn't afford to be alone anymore. "You have suggestions," Hạc Cúc said.

"I don't!" Nhi said. "I'm just—"

"Smart," Hạc Cúc said. "Fast. Adaptable."

"None of this—"

Hạc Cúc could almost feel Nhi shivering at her side, trying to get a grip on things. "Yes," she said. "It is helping. Because you know what to do."

"As if!" And a slow exhale from Nhi. "She's behind the tangler, isn't she? It's so huge it's distorting the sensors' input."

"We could go above it," Lành said. She sounded as if she was going to be sick. How long did they have before she turned tail, the same way she always did?

Nhi said, "You're not going anywhere. You're staying here."

"I told you I don't need your pity!"

Nhi's voice was dry and merciless. "I don't provide pity. I provide orders. You're staying here, and—" On the comms, a map flashed, briefly. "This is where you're deploying your barrier generators. Hạc Cúc and I are going to find Bảo Duy."

Hạc Cúc looked at the map. Lành's barrier generators formed the first quarter of a loose sphere, at the back and towards the bottom of the tangler. She said, "You want us to go on either side, I take it. At the very edge of the tendrils. It's going to be very tight, timewise." After they finished their quarter of the sphere around the tangler, they were going to need to do the most difficult one: the one that was partly in front—wherever Bảo Duy had disappeared to.

Hạc Cúc tried not to worry about Bảo Duy. She didn't feel Nhi's sense of responsibility towards the other members of the team, but they needed the Rat because there weren't enough of them, or enough skills among them, and Bảo Duy hadn't exactly come across as someone who'd keep away from danger.

"Yes," Nhi said. Another command, one she took on faith that Hạc Cúc would obey. And she knew, didn't she? She knew that Hạc Cúc might hate this mission to the guts, but that, in the end, she would do everything in her power to make sure it succeeded. Because it was everything her sư phụ had taught her: do what is right, and do it right.

"Let's do this," Hạc Cúc said, grimly, and pushed the nose of her glider up and to the right, just as Nhi pushed hers to the left and up, without a further word spoken. She watched Nhi on the other side—half-tempted to press herself further against the invisible tendrils to be closer to Nhi, knowing it would be utterly unreasonable to do so.

There was silence, on the comm. Lành, chastened, obviously didn't feel like talking. And Hạc Cúc wanted the focus—that relentless, sharp sense of meaning it brought to everything, the feeling of being alive, of cutting through the skin of the world until it bled. They were going to try and trap the tangler, and when they had it . . . it was going to be over, one way or another. Her way of making a difference.

As she angled upwards, dropping barrier generators

behind her, she sent short, fast bursts of Divine Harmony Shadow into the darkness to her left. She'd caught glimpses of Nhi as they went further in—and then nothing more, but the pressure she felt in answer to her own Shadow grew and grew, no longer a little nibbling at the edges of what she held, but a continuous wall that pressed against her. With each burst, she pushed it back, but it would push back in turn—and each burst drained her further, the life-energy circulating within her body's meridians being tapped further and further to keep projecting her Shadow.

That tangler was *huge*. It couldn't possibly be only six measures. She'd been going for so long now, and there was nothing but unrelenting pressure—that sharp, inescapable knowledge that the moment she ran out of Shadow, she'd be overwhelmed and stung, and in such a narrow space, not even Nhi could save her.

Not even Nhi. And realistically, why was she expecting anything of Nhi? They barely knew each other; she barely trusted Nhi. And yet. And yet. Somewhere in her heart of hearts was the absolute belief that, just as Nhi had expected her trust, she in turn had given hers to Nhi. It was . . . sobering. Wrong.

Where was Bảo Duy?

Hạc Cúc was alone in the darkness with just that relentless push against her Shadow, nightmare flashes in her brain of all the navigators she'd seen lost to tanglers—bumping into things, continuously forgetting what they had been doing, focusing with difficulty, struggling for speech in slurred words—and at the end, choking on their own lack of breath. She was alone, with the inescapable knowledge she wasn't Quang Lộc, that she would never be Quang

Lộc—too abrasive, too unkind, too unskilled, with none of the gentle diplomacy and impeccable navigator arts that had brought him so much face among the clans. The tangler pressed against her again. Startled, she lost control of her Shadow and felt it cave in, the tendrils going straight to her face. In panic, she flailed, the glider starting to spin—which just made it worse, setting it on a collision course with the tangler to her right—more pressure on her disintegrating shields, her breathing becoming shorter and shorter, everything narrowing to brief, jagged moments.

The tendrils, going past her face and into the void. The glider, spinning as Hạc Cúc struggled to regain control of it. Why were the commands not answering, why—? The mass to her right, crushing her. Her Shadow, slipping out of her hands, desperately trying to summon something, anything—

"Chị." It was Nhi's voice, crackling and oddly distorted. The comms. She said something Hạc Cúc couldn't hear, and then, "Remember when you told me I had this? You have, too." There was absolute certainty in her voice.

Hạc Cúc wanted to scoff. What could Nhi possibly know about her, about any of her?

"Breathe," Nhi said, simply.

Breathing? As if breathing would help. She'd prove Nhi wrong. Hạc Cúc breathed in, slowly. One two three four five, one two three four five . . . The viscous, persistent pressing on her Shadow didn't go away—but her hands, fumbling with the glider, nudged it out of its spin. The glider stabilized, shuddering. Hạc Cúc put the thrusters into higher speed—she'd run out of fuel but she needed to get away, and *fast*. The glider trembled under her—for a single, desperate moment she saw how the future would be: the thrust not powerful enough to move away from the tangler, the inexorable collapse of her defenses, and the multitude of stings that would end her there and then. At least it would be swift, which was no comfort at all.

And then—like a knife tearing itself from flesh—the glider sped away from the huge body trying to snare her. The view in front of her opened to her Shadow; she'd moved past the tangler.

Hạc Cúc breathed, fast and ragged, trying to still the frantic beating of her heart. She slowed her glider so she'd remain in front of the tangler—it was moving at about five paces per centiday, the clip of a clan ship at low speed. Her Shadow quivered and contracted, uncontrolled. She folded it. The memory of that tendril, going for her face . . . no. No time for this. She keyed up the positions of the barrier generators; there was a slightly larger gap where she'd lost control, but still within the parameters Bảo Duy had given them.

Speaking of Bảo Duy . . .

Hạc Cúc still couldn't see her anywhere. Just the darkness of the canyon: ahead of her, it veered sharply to the left, becoming shallower and narrower, with more and more jagged outcrops. Which meant they wouldn't have as much margin to drop the barrier generators in front of the tangler. They needed to end this, and fast.

Where was Bảo Duy?

"How are you?" It was Nhi. She'd come out her side, glider shining under the unwavering light of the stars. Behind her loomed the shape of the Ice Jade Planet.

"How am I? Not good," Hạc Cúc said, curtly. "Can we talk about this later? We need to complete setting up the generators. And to find Bảo Duy. Have you heard from Lành?" She'd been silent on the comms.

"I have," Nhi said. "About an eighth centiday ago. She was almost done. Very visibly ill at ease, but otherwise doing reasonably well."

It made Hạc Cúc unbelievably, irrationally angry—how dare Lành be so brave in the face of her worst fears, when all Hạc Cúc herself had managed was losing control and almost getting killed by a tangler?

"There's just this quarter of the sphere to cover now."

"Hmm," Nhi said. "Shall we split? One person for the barrier generators, one to find her."

"I thought you were in charge."

"Maybe. But you could use some control over things."

She could. Having a reassurance that some part of the universe could be, if not predictable, at least something she could act on. Something she could kill. "No," she said. "Barrier generators first." She tried to hold up a hand to forestall Nhi's objections, remembered the magnetic clamps holding her to the glider and preventing that gesture. "We need to stop it. I can't see Bảo Duy. I don't know what the emergency with her is, so I have to make that choice based on what is in front of me."

Nhi was silent for a while. "Yes. I agree. Let's do this." And she angled her glider down and towards the front of the tangler. Hạc Cúc took a deep breath—every nerve in her body tingled at the prospect of willingly putting herself close to the tangler again—and followed her, braced for that viscous touch on her Shadow.

They worked in silence, moving like dancers to some unheard music. The tangler was quiescent; there were no tendrils in front, but the bulk of its mass pressed against their feet and legs, a reminder of what could happen if they failed.

Hạc Cúc was dropping off the third-to-last generator when Nhi said, "Here."

"What?"

It was just a glint of silver on one of the outcroppings, ahead to the right—by the side of an abandoned dome in a horizontal position. It had long since cracked open. "You can't know—" Hạc Cúc said.

"It's the exact color of our suits," Nhi said, in a tone that brooked no argument. A hesitation. "There's just two generators left, one for each of us. Can you—"

Hạc Cúc fought the entirely unfair panic at the prospect of being left alone with the tangler again. "Yes," she said. "I can drop yours off, too. Why don't you pass it to me?"

Nhi glided closer—close enough to touch. Her generator attached itself to Hạc Cúc's glider—and then she did reach out, one gloved hand gently lingering on Hạc Cúc's arm. Hạc Cúc found her breath catching in her chest.

"Ancestors' luck be with you," Nhi said, and Hạc Cúc found herself at a complete loss for words as Nhi left.

"You too!" she said finally, even though Nhi was by now a smaller shape accelerating towards the outcropping. She'd done something to her Shadow, something that made her smaller and less visible, the same kind of thing she did to her body posture when she was nervous, fading into the background when she should have been gloriously there.

"Always," Nhi said, and Hạc Cúc didn't need to see her to imagine the smile on her face. It did odd things to her chest, twisting some organs whose existence she'd been barely aware of before.

This woman. This impossible, infuriating woman. Hạc Cúc felt herself smiling again as she dropped off the two barrier generators, and they locked onto the tangler. Done.

Nothing happened.

"Em?" she said.

"I'm a bit busy," Nhi said. "Can't really navigate those rocks and talk to you."

"It doesn't seem to be working." Hạc Cúc fought the panic in her throat. "You did drop your generators?"

A silence.

"Of course I did."

Lành. She ought to have known she couldn't trust Lành. "Em," she said to Lành on the comms. "Em, please come in."

"I see her," Nhi said. Her voice came in distantly, and clearly worried. "Bảo Duy. She's been stung, and she's under some kind of rock fall. I need to get her clear."

Not good. Not good.

Breathe. She could deal with that kind of emergency. She needed to, no matter how dire it seemed. "You get her out," she said to Nhi. "I'm going to locate Lành."

"Yes," Nhi said. And, with that faint touch of amusement to her voice, "Please try to keep Lành alive, if you can."

If she could. Hạc Cúc turned around, and plunged under the tangler.

It was, like them on their gliders, mostly horizontal in the direction of its flight, the umbrella in front with most of its tendrils trailing behind it. Beneath it, there was just the pressure on her Shadow—and an absolute and total lack of barrier generators in what should have been the last quarter of the sphere.

"Em," she said to Lành again. "Come in."

How had she been so lacking in common sense, how had she been so trusting? She ought to have known she couldn't trust Lành. That, at heart, Lành was just this broken child her sư phụ had taken pity on, but that ultimately the flaw at her heart would always surface, always betray her and everyone with her.

"Em!"

Naive, naive, naive. She ought to have known better, but for a moment she'd allowed herself to believe the same way Nhi had believed—Nhi, who knew too much and still chose to trust, or at any rate to work with what she had.

"Em!"

Hạc Cúc sent a burst of Shadow angling towards the back of the tangler—for a moment, she saw it clearly: the massiveness of it, the impossibly large pulsing mass with tendrils spreading, forming an impassable corona at the back, a glistening net that would snare her and never let go . . .

Focus. Focus.

There was a smaller mass ahead of the corona, a little knot of tendrils tightly wrapped around something.

Her heart sank.

"Em," she said, not believing Lành was going to come in anymore.

As Hạc Cúc cautiously angled closer, she saw that it was indeed Lành. She was hanging from her immobile glider, and yet she was moving, her body horizontal with the momentum. Hạc Cúc couldn't see her face with the suit's visor on, but the whole pose felt off—it wasn't just the muscle re-laxation, but something that felt to Hạc Cúc almost like ec-stasy, the way some bodhisattva were depicted in temples. Something that definitely had no place here, in the midst of a tangler's corona. Hạc Cúc sent another burst of Shadow, heedless of the way it made her whole body shudder with fatigue, and saw that the tendrils were parting around Lành, forming a loose cage. So, not stung. Or maybe already stung and being dragged into the umbrella to be digested? But no, she didn't seem to be moving further into the tangler. She was just hanging there, keeping pace with it.

And if that wasn't the most absolutely disturbing and creepy thing.

"Wake up," Hạc Cúc said. "Wake up!!"

She'd managed to drop barrier generators before being caught; there was just one missing, and Hạc Cúc—like everyone else—had had spare ones for redundancy. She could easily drop it into place. Well, not easily, necessarily, but it could be done. The issue was that if she did that, she'd trap Lành in with the tangler.

She considered it, briefly. It was certainly expedient. Pragmatic, compared to the option of failure. And Snakes had always been the pragmatic, expedient ones. She'd ask herself what Quang Lộc would do, but he would advise her to be merciful, to stand up for Lành as he'd done. To forgive her.

She stared at Lành, trailing within the tangler. She hated Lành's guts, but there was a difference between that and leaving her to die. Hạc Cúc lived by a code, which wasn't the Snakes': she knew what mattered was protect-ing those who couldn't protect themselves. And failing at

the mission—as she'd always known Lành would do—
wasn't the same thing as being guilty of anything. If being
cowardly or having no principles was a criteria on which
to assassinate people, Hạc Cúc would have killed half of
humanity already.

She fiddled with the barrier generator. By her calcula-
tions, she had about two-eighths of a centiday—so a quarter
centiday—before the barrier generators lost the lock on the
tangler. It was going to be difficult. Very difficult.

"How are you doing?" she asked Nhi.

A grunt, from the comms. "Can't. Talk. Now."

Right. So it was just her, then.

Nhi's voice, in her head. *You can do it.*

Of course she could, or at the very least she could prove
Nhi wrong.

She set her comms to send a high-pitched, unpleasant
sound calibrated to keep people from sleeping. Not that
she thought it would get Lành back from wherever Lành
was, but it might prevent her from being snared again.

Then she set her glider to dive, and gathered her Shadow
to her, concentrating the gathered energy into a focused,
lethal burst that she usually used to push off assailants and
finish them off. As she got closer and closer to the tangler,
she felt the push of it. The slimy feeling of something that
was going to shatter her—except it was oddly muted, because these tendrils were centered on Lành and not her.

And wasn't that a thing she absolutely refused to think
about until everyone was safe.

As she got closer—close enough to touch, close enough
to be stung—Hạc Cúc sent her burst into the mass of tendrils. It left her with the feeling of something tearing inside

her—and the tendrils recoiled as if she'd hurt them. In the brief moment when she could still see them, in the sharpened contrast that came in the wake of her Shadow, Hạc Cúc swooped down, and grabbed Lành—and veered away sharply once more, away from the tendrils. She unfolded her Shadow again as she did so, and it was all pressure now, all mindless will to take her and crush her—and she wasn't going to make it, she was going to have to let go of her Shadow, they would both die here, now . . .

Then she was clear, Lành still limp behind her, trailing on the momentum of Hạc Cúc's glider. Hạc Cúc wanted to shake her, but now wasn't the time. Now, she needed to make sure the tangler was trapped, or her stunt would all have been for nothing.

At her back, the pressure on her Shadow—now deployed to protect Lành—increased. There was a sound, overlaying and merging with the one she'd put on to wake Lành up—some kind of primal and unpleasant scream, like fear, like rage, like pain. Lành shuddered and moved.

"What—what's going on?" Her voice was heavy with something Hạc Cúc couldn't quite name.

"Not now," Hạc Cúc said. She was steering, racing towards that last hole in the sphere of barrier generators, even as the pressure on them increased. She held on, grimly, shaking. One measure left. Half a measure. A quarter. She could barely see, everything was narrowing and turning black. Too much drawing on reserves she no longer had. She—

There.

She dropped off the last of the barrier generators. There was an audible click on her comms—a held, shaking breath when she feared they'd missed the deadline—but then they all activated at once, forming a sphere of shimmering light. The pressure on her Shadow vanished as if it had never been; the shock of it almost sent her tumbling away from her glider, which would have been bad as she had no personal thrusters and no way to recover in the vacuum of space.

"I've got Lành," she said to Nhi on the comms.

"And the tangler, I see," Nhi said. "I've got Bảo Duy, but she's unconscious. Well done. Now we need to kill—"

Hạc Cúc cut her off before she could speak further. "That requires knowledge from one unconscious Rat. Or more people who aren't utterly exhausted. We're leaving it here and calling in the elders. They'll deal with it."

"Can you turn off that irritating noise?" Lành asked, sharply. She was awake and being utterly unpleasant. Well, the usual, then.

Hạc Cúc smiled. "As you wish," she said, tempted for half a moment to turn it all the way up. But she cut it, and turned the glider around, ready to fly back to the shuttle. As she did so, she saw all of the tangler, twisting and turning in the sphere that now kept it imprisoned: a huge mass of darker lights against the light of the barrier, tendrils weaving in slow and utterly alien movements. And she knew, instinctively, that it wasn't going to be over until it was dead, except they had no means and few ideas on how to kill it.

5

SECRETS

"That was very well done," Elder Liễu said.

She'd arrived at the inn with a delegation of other Elders from the Council of the Eight: an elderly Rat woman, a middle-aged, plump Snake Hạc Cúc had seemed to dislike on sight, and a startlingly young Ox who'd immediately and bossily taken charge. Nhi knew them on sight—everyone knew the Council of the Eight—but didn't know enough about them, and the thought of having to talk to total strangers made her weak in the knees.

There'd been no sign of a Dog anywhere, which was odd. Something was itching at the back of Nhi's mind, something she couldn't quite place: that feeling that secrets didn't quite make sense, that she was missing something that would make everything fall into place.

Elder Liễu had received Nhi alone, which was clearly in deference to Nhi's personal preferences. The others were with the Council: Bảo Duy, chastened and bandaged; Lành, aggressive, unpleasant, unwilling to talk about any of what had happened to her; Hạc Cúc, exhausted and disinclined to explain anything. Nhi hoped they would be all right, but she couldn't be sure.

There was tea on the table, and translucent dumplings

with shrimps. Nhi picked at hers with her chopsticks, trying to breathe.

"We'll deal with the tangler," Elder Liễu was saying. She was sitting between the two energy-founts in the room: all the shining blue lines converged to her, putting her wrinkled, sharp face in darkness and making her seem like something from the oldest stories, a wise woman scholar, or a statue of a bodhisattva.

"And the others?" Nhi said. "The strobilation."

"That's going to take more time," Elder Liễu said, smoothly. A sigh. "You know there are politics in the Council."

Of course. That didn't mean Nhi appreciated them. "Yes," she said. "Is this your way of telling me you're not going to deal with the remaining tangler seeds? The other juniors and I can take care of them."

"You," Elder Liễu said, sharply, "need to be in the infirmary."

"That's Bảo Duy," Nhi said. Bảo Duy had sheepishly apologized for going off on her own—as Nhi had suspected, she'd wanted to observe the tangler alone. She'd deliberately left the barrier generators behind her to not be a hindrance. Nhi supposed she should at least give Bảo Duy credit for not wanting to put the other juniors in danger. Minor credit for that, major discredit for endangering the entire mission.

Elder Liễu knew Nhi well enough to know that when exhausted and stressed, she became literal and blunt. She had the grace to not say anything about disrespect. "You'll owe me a full accounting," she said. "But it can wait until you're all recovered. Most juniors wouldn't have done half as well as you did."

"Is that why you sent us?" Nhi said. That feeling of unease again. "Politics?"

Elder Liễu grimaced. "It's for the good of the clans," she said, finally.

Which wasn't an answer.

A sigh, from her. "I'll send people to deal with the strobilating tanglers, one way or another. You have my word. We wouldn't want any loss of life in the Silver Stream." Behind her, the Ice Jade Planet rose, all green and blue, none of the huge arcologies on its surface visible from this height.

Nhi considered it. Elder Liễu's word, like Nhi's, wasn't given lightly. "There's something you're not telling me," she said. She clung to her Shadow, but it was weak and trembling, and not as comforting as it should be. She was exhausted from the tangler chase, and from having to pull Bảo Duy out from under the rocks that had collapsed on her. Rats. Definitely couldn't be trusted with common sense. Bảo Duy had thought a tangler observation project was more important than anything else, even her own life.

"Yes," Elder Liễu said. "You'll have to trust me on this."

And Nhi did. Except . . . "What about Ly Châu?"

"Mmm." Elder Liễu sighed. "I want to wait until we've dealt with the tangler to deal with Ly Châu. Right now it's imprisoned by your barrier, but neither Elder Hạnh from the Rat clan nor Elder Ánh Ngọc from the Snake have figured out how to damage it in the least."

Ah. Nhi could see some of the shape of it, perhaps: that it was a loss of face for the clans if they were unable to deal with a tangler. That the imperial clan would love to see them admit weakness, to finally claim dominance over navigation and the steady stream of income it provided. "I see," she said. "Do you need help?" It felt presumptuous, but it was sincerely offered, which was the only thing Nhi had in her anymore.

"No," Elder Liễu said, sternly. "I need you to rest, and then you and the others can coordinate the juniors who'll arrive to deal with the tangler seeds from the strobilation. We'll deal with the large one."

She sounded utterly confident, and bossy: the mother Nhi barely remembered, the one who'd died in mysterious circumstances—the one terrible and unattainable secret of Nhi's life, the thing all other secrets were proxies for. The thing that was forever beyond reach, her parents' corpses inaccessible in the wilderness where they'd died, the clan's best efforts uncovering no evidence or testimonies. The thing that she feared most and yet would never have an explanation for. An onslaught of utter fatigue and panic assaulted her, everything she'd been keeping at bay suddenly coming into sharp and unbearable focus, even Elder Liễu's voice resonating painfully under the metal ceilings of the habitats. She was sitting too close to Nhi, talking too loudly—every clink of her cup was too much, an echo that felt like it was drilling into Nhi's brain. "I have to go," Nhi said. "Thank you for your time."

She rose, shakily—on the verge of utterly coming apart—clinging to her diminished Shadow like a faltering lifeline.

Hạc Cúc. She needed Hạc Cúc's company now.

Hạc Cúc couldn't sleep. They were done with the Council of the Eight, an utterly draining, exhausting, and pointless exercise that had seen way too much posturing and way too much infighting among the clans, with the juniors' decisions scrutinized and criticized as a proxy for gaining political points—all the bickering and infighting her sư phụ Quang Lộc effortlessly navigated and for which she had so little patience. Yet another reason why she wouldn't ever be worthy of him.

Frustrated, exhausted, and acutely conscious she was a finger's width from snapping at someone or stabbing them or both, Hạc Cúc wandered down the corridors of the inn the Council of the Eight had commandeered. It was not the same one they'd stayed in with Ly Châu, but it was similar enough: a series of small rooms with large openings onto the Silver Stream and its chaotically oriented buildings and ballet of shuttles that never really seemed to slow down— and the Ice Jade Planet in the background like a huge, dim sun, the contours of its continents sharply outlined.

A ping on her comms. It was Nhi. "Em, what's going on?"

No answer from Nhi.

"Em?"

"Chị." It was Nhi on her comms. She sounded exhausted and wrung out, on the verge of panic. "Please. Help."

Hạc Cúc felt as though she'd been thrown out into space, instantly going from exhausted and annoyed to keyed up. Sharp and all too aware she'd pay for it one way or another. "What's happening?"

No answer. And, finally, "Help."

Help. Hạc Cúc ran through a dozen scenarios in her mind, and discarded them all. The elders from all the clans were there, which meant no tangler or assassin would get into the inn. The most likely explanation was fallout from Nhi's interview with her own clan elder, which she had no way of guessing at. Each clan's politics were their own.

"Where are you?"

"Room," Nhi said.

Room. A different room. The Council of the Eight had drawn the usual boundaries between clans: instead of the juniors rooming together, they now had rooms in separate clan quarters. Which meant Rooster territory.

"I'm coming," she said. She struggled to think of something that would be reassuring—decidedly not her specialty—and everything she could think of seemed false or insincere. "I'm coming," she said, again.

She followed the string of small rooms with open doors—the tearooms all lit up, the blinking blue lines of energy, the sharp smell of jasmine tea, the narrow openings and their ballet of shuttles carrying people from angled building to angled building. The private quarters: fewer people, doors locked or with retainers or alarms set on them. Ox. Rat. Snake.

There.

There was no sign. No alarm. But Shadow within, that she could feel even without unfolding her own very far, a brash and steady presence that belonged to the Roosters—not Nhi's, which was far more cautious.

Hạc Cúc unfolded her own Shadow, not very far, not very strong, but just enough to signal her own presence, and that she wasn't going to budge a single finger's width, no matter what happened. Then she walked in. Not running—because that was going to be nothing but trouble in quarters full of another clan. Just walking at a fast enough clip, trying not to think of Nhi and what kind of trouble she could have gotten into.

I'm coming. I'm coming. I'm coming.

Stay where you are. Please. Please.

"Can I help you?" It was a Rooster junior, the sort of vaguely familiar face from clan conclaves.

Hạc Cúc smiled. "That's all right," she said. She kept her Shadow under control. It took an effort. She was exhausted. "I'm just looking for Nhi. I needed to go over something with her." She kept her voice even, her tone casual.

"Ah." The Rooster junior stared at her for a moment, trying to decide if it was worth their while to challenge her. Hạc Cúc felt their Shadow bump against hers, probing to see if there was any give. "I see. She's that way."

"Thank you." Hạc Cúc was too tired for this. For any of this.

It was all Rooster colors: jewel tones, brash green the color of imperial jade, the deep blue of Heaven's cloth, the decoration a mixture of vids projected on configurable decoration-screens and of cloths that must have come with the elders, a far cry from the bare rooms the juniors had had to make do with—a riot of unsubtle, almost tasteless decoration that reminded Hạc Cúc of why Roosters in general got on her nerves fairly fast.

She found Nhi in one of the smaller rooms: a bed and barely enough space around it to stand, and that same riot of colors all around, though the screens were off. Nhi herself was on the bed, barely visible under the quilt, Shadow so tightly wrapped around her it felt like an impregnable ship.

"I'm here," Hạc Cúc said. "Em?"

No answer from the bed. Hạc Cúc unfolded her Shadow a little more, feeling, acutely, the connection between her vitality center—the place low in her belly where the Shadow coalesced—and everything she was extending towards Nhi.

Still no answer.

"Em."

Bodily, Hạc Cúc had an intense desire to scream or do something nonsensical. She was either too late or she wasn't—a straightforward, calm logic she'd applied all her life to most scenarios but whose cold sharpness now deserted her in the moment she needed it most.

Think think think. Panic or self-recrimination were *not* going to help. Unfortunately, her brain hadn't gotten the message, and was currently busy indulging in both. She could have run on her way here. She should have run.

She—

Against her own Shadow, something small flickered. "Em."

In a heartbeat she was on the bed, kneeling by Nhi's side. A hand poked out, held hers—and squeezed. She squeezed back. For a moment there was nothing in the entire universe but that shock of warm flesh against hers, that frantic heartbeat, a faint flicker in Nhi's Shadow.

She wanted to ask what happened, who she should stab. She held herself still, and asked, instead, slowly and softly, "What do you need?"

A silence. Nhi's Shadow, quietly and softly pulsing. "Silence," she said, and it was almost inaudible.

Ah.

Hạc Cúc stared at the turned-off screens, and then back at Nhi. So not just silence, but possibly also darkness. "Give me a moment," she said. She got up and turned off the energy-fount in the room. The glowing blue lines vanished; the room turned darker, and the slight buzzing sound of the energy-fount vanished from hearing. She walked back to sit next to Nhi, grabbed the hand that was offered to her again, and waited. She said nothing, just felt their Shadows next to each other. Slowly and carefully, Hạc Cúc stretched her own Shadow further and further. Nhi's Shadow, slow and cautious, surged to meet it; they twined, like their stretched hands. Hạc Cúc closed her eyes and imagined herself flying: she was in her own clan ship, *The Steel Clam*, a sleek and small craft that could only carry five or six passengers and their cargo. She was moving in the Hollows, outracing any tanglers—maneuvering fast, the ship feeling like an extension of her own Shadow, sleek and fast and veering through the starless void of the Hollows, the space that twisted all light into darkness and all sound into scattered meaninglessness. She was sharp and fast and everything she needed to be—everything *Nhi* needed. She could feel Nhi, on the edge of her own Shadow—felt the moment Nhi's own Shadow slowly withdrew.

She opened her eyes. Nhi was sitting on the bed, staring at her. She had circles under her eyes, and looked like she hadn't slept in days. To be honest, she probably hadn't. Neither of them had.

"Thank you," Nhi said.

Hạc Cúc sniffed. "For what?"

There was a long silence, Nhi's face hardening. Hạc Cúc saw it as clear as a tangler in the Hollows: she was going to push Hạc Cúc away again. And it would have been fine, if she hadn't looked so tired. If she hadn't looked like she could use the help, and the company. Hạc Cúc said, instead, "Would you like to tell me about secrets?"

Nhi's face softened. Hạc Cúc moved closer to her—and Nhi did the same thing, until they sat side by side on the bed. "There are too many," she said. Her voice was still shaking.

"Among the juniors?"

"No," Nhi said. She folded, her face resting on Hạc Cúc's shoulder. Hạc Cúc felt a great, unfamiliar, and almost embarrassing warmth deep in her chest; she'd been physical and even close with her girlfriends in the past, but she'd never experienced anything as devastatingly intimate and vulnerable as this.

"Ah. The elders, then. I'm assuming it's not the tangler." She paused. "Sorry. I'm tired, and it makes it hard not to be sarcastic."

Nhi didn't speak for a while, or move. Hạc Cúc felt the weight of her head on her shoulder, the slow and steady rhythm of her breath, everything she wanted to keep and hold forever.

"When I'm tired," Nhi said, slowly, carefully, "everything seems to jumble together. Things get too loud, too bright. And I—" Another silence. "I feel like something terrible will happen if I don't get to my own rooms immediately."

She said it like it was a shameful secret. Hạc Cúc chewed

on it like a valued confidence. She said, matter-of-factly, "What kind of terrible thing?"

"That I'll lash out at everyone with Shadow, or collapse inwards and never recover. And in the moment, I'm not sure which is worse."

"They're both equally bad," Hạc Cúc said, sharply. "You know you're not worth *less* than other people, don't you?"

A sigh, from Nhi. "Sometimes."

Hạc Cúc's heart felt too large for her chest. At least it was honest, but it made her angry that Nhi didn't value herself more. There were plenty of terrible people in this life, and they wholeheartedly believed themselves to be better than others—and Nhi, who was someone, didn't believe in herself enough. "I'll take that," Hạc Cúc said. "But we should come back to it."

"Maybe," Nhi said.

"Did something terrible ever happen to you?"

"I don't know," Nhi said. It was bare and honest. "Maybe it did, when I was a child and less able to deal with it. Maybe it didn't."

"You're not always able to get to your own rooms, are you?"

"Sometimes I just run," Nhi said. "As far as I can. As fast as I can. So I can be somewhere in the silence and try to hold it all at bay."

"I'm assuming that's what happened just now," Hạc Cúc said. A silence. She reached out to squeeze Nhi's hand. "How secret is it?"

Nhi said, "The kind of thing that would be embarrassing to admit to an elder, let alone to other clans."

Hạc Cúc laughed, softly. "Good thing I'm not that kind of other clan, then."

"Chị!"

"I know what you mean," Hạc Cúc said, more seriously. She said, finally, "I appreciate the trust." She chewed on it for a while, wondering on what would be fair to give in return. She said, finally, "I'm always afraid."

"You?" Nhi snorted. "You—"

Hạc Cúc put a finger on Nhi's lips—feeling them contract under her touch, sending a spike of breathless, heightened desire within her. "Shh," she said. "Not of people. Of myself."

"Ah." Nhi's words were barely audible beneath Hạc Cúc's touch.

Hạc Cúc said, slowly, carefully, "I was five when Quang Lộc chose me. He walked among the Snake younglings, the ones barely old enough to be disciples, and he pointed to me. He said I would do great things."

"You have." There was quiet wonder in Nhi's voice. It hurt, because she didn't know what she was talking about.

"No," Hạc Cúc said. "I'm too brash. Too sharp. Too cruel. You've seen it with Lành."

"Lành would drive anyone to anger." An exhausted sigh from Nhi. "And she's been even worse than usual on this mission."

"Not my sư phụ," Hạc Cúc said, simply. "And I'll never be him."

Nhi was silent for a while. She slid from Hạc Cúc's shoulder, down into her lap. Her face—bruised, dark, and haggard—looked up at Hạc Cúc. Even worn down and shaking, she was still the loveliest person Hạc Cúc had seen; there was something about her that just drew her eye and held it, a quiet firmness, a deliberation, a sense that she wholly inhabited the space around her and wouldn't ever twist herself out of shape to conform to what others expected. She was frowning now, looking away from Hạc Cúc, but her attention was still utterly focused on her, so strong Hạc Cúc could almost feel the air trembling with it. Hạc Cúc shivered with anticipation, with a wild and nebulous desire to bend down, to touch Nhi. She held herself still instead, because the last thing Nhi needed was someone invading her space now.

Finally Nhi said, "It must be so hard, feeling you need to be perfect all the time, else it'll all come apart at any point." Each word felt like it had been weighed, carefully slotted into its proper place.

Hạc Cúc had expected some of the same platitudes people had told her—things about being her own self, about how it didn't and shouldn't matter. She'd been bracing herself against hearing them from Nhi's mouth. Instead . . . instead, she had this, and it was like a shock in her chest. An odd, discomfiting thrill, the same thing she'd felt when they'd touched back on the shuttle.

"Yes," she said. "Yes." She grasped for words that wouldn't come. She was in shock, and it was ridiculous. She killed people for a living. She'd imprisoned the largest tangler ever seen. She shouldn't have been struck speechless.

Nhi reached up. She was surrounded by Shadow—it spread around her like a halo, but Hạc Cúc saw now that Nhi used it as a shield to steady herself against the world. "Chị?" she said.

"Yes?"

Nhi drew her down, and kissed her.

Her lips were warm and trembling under Hạc Cúc's—and the wave of desire within her crested and hardened, and she kissed Nhi back, feeling at once too tight and too large for her own body, that sense of warmth tightening in her lower belly, Shadow flaring for a brief moment.

Nhi broke the kiss, but didn't run away like she had on the shuttle. She remained in Hạc Cúc's lap, staring up at her. Smiling, and it was an expression Hạc Cúc would have killed again and again to see.

"Thank you," Hạc Cúc said.

Nhi laughed. "For what?" she said, asking exactly the question Hạc Cúc had asked of her, earlier, but it was softer and quieter, and there was affection in it.

"Nothing," Hạc Cúc said. She felt herself blush. "Secrets."

"Now that would be worth something," Nhi said. "Speaking of secrets—"

"Shh. Not now," Hạc Cúc said—and bent down and kissed Nhi again, because she could.

After the kiss—the kisses—Nhi remained on her bed, staring at the ceiling. She rubbed her own skin, feeling the warmth in her belly and cheeks. She felt boneless and drained, but it wasn't altogether an unpleasant feeling. She wanted to sink into sleep with the memory of Hạc Cúc's touch on her lips, the slight press of Hạc Cúc's skin on her—wondering what it'd feel like to feel that press elsewhere.

And, beyond the kisses, there had been what they had shared. Time together. Space. Not just physical space, but mental space. Intimacy. Hạc Cúc asking what Nhi needed. Listening to Nhi's own secrets—to shameful things, and not blinking, not judging. Simply listening and asking questions, trying to get to the bottom of how it all worked, taking it all on faith. And, most of all, she'd offered a secret in return, understanding the weight of what Nhi was offering her.

Nhi hoped she'd said the right words in exchange for that secret—Hạc Cúc had let her kiss her, and even kissed Nhi again, which surely meant it hadn't been such a terrible thing to say in return. Surely she'd have said, if Nhi had offended?

Surely.

The weight of the exhaustion Nhi had been keeping at bay was coming back now, crushing her. The deep-seated knowledge that holding secrets—that speaking up while knowing them—was bound to drive people away. That it might be safer, and more convenient, to drive Hạc Cúc away before they both got too attached and got hurt. No matter how much she wanted this.

As Nhi lay on the bed staring at the darkened ceiling, feeling her own thoughts scatter and peter out, the Shadow she'd wrapped around her for pressure slowly fading away as her conscious control slipped, things surfaced in and out of existence. Events and facts, fizzing in and out. Ly Châu. Nebula Cinnabar. A navigator poison, slow acting. No Dog among the elders, and that curious deflection from Elder Liễu about politics. The tangler, too huge, too frightening. Juniors. Bảo Duy, too inclined to gamble her own life away. Lành, bitter and uncontrollable. Hạc Cúc, isolated and overaggressive. Nhi, asocial, graceless, slow. All of them failures in their own different ways.

Failures. Expected to fail. Expendable.

This had never been about catching a tangler, and people were in danger. No, not just people. The clans. Everyone.

She needed to warn someone.

But darkness was catching up to her, and she sank into sleep, powerless to stop it.

6

FIGHTS

Hạc Cúc walked away from Nhi's room with a smile on her face and a deep feeling of satiation and happiness with the world that lasted all of five blinks—until she remembered exactly the situation she was in. In the Rooster quarters of an inn with a tangler still to be dealt with, far too much politics, and no immediate escape from any of it.

Not to mention Nhi.

It had been good, with Nhi. A space to be someone she usually wasn't. To not have to excel. Nhi had got it exactly right when she'd said that it felt like it was all tearing her apart.

Except Nhi was wrong, too. She hadn't seen all of Hạc Cúc. Deep down, Hạc Cúc was sure that Nhi, like the rest of her girlfriends, hoped that Hạc Cúc was like her sư phụ, Quang Lộc—compassionate and kind in addition to her navigator skills.

And Hạc Cúc knew—deep down, deep in her heart—that she would never attain the same space as her sư phụ. That she would never live up to the promise she'd shown when she'd been chosen. Nhi would inevitably see that.

Tea. She needed tea. She'd find some tea and just enjoy it there, staring at space. Looking at the unblinking stars and enjoying their slow, invisible changes. Yes.

She wandered into the first room with an open door:

a long, narrow one, its large opening showing the Ice Jade Planet, its continents sharply delineated beneath whirls of clouds. Hạc Cúc almost turned back, startled, because there was someone seated there already, the lines of energy converging on a table and a tray—and when that someone rose, Hạc Cúc saw that it was Lành.

They stared at each other for a while.

"Joining me for a drink?" Lành's voice was bitter, but the offer seemed sincere. Hạc Cúc hesitated. "Of course you won't."

Hạc Cúc wasn't sure, later, what pushed her further into the room: a mixture of curiosity and need for company, even if that company was someone she utterly despised. A hunger for a connection to Quang Lộc, no matter its cause.

Lành poured the tea, handed one to Hạc Cúc. Her Shadow was weak, pulsing in odd patterns, unlike the quiet brashness of Ambush in the Grass. There were deep circles under her eyes, and something else: a fey light that reminded Hạc Cúc of the tangler's tendrils, contrasted with Shadow.

"I suppose I should thank you," Lành said. "For rescuing me."

Hạc Cúc raised an eyebrow. "Your gratitude is overwhelming."

"Don't make this more difficult than it already is. I put up with Nhi because she means well. I'm not sure why I put up with you at all," Lành snapped. She downed her tea in one gulp, as if it had been rice wine. She stared at the empty cup, her silhouette dwarfed by the Ice Jade Planet behind her. "It spoke to me," she said, softly, slowly. "I can still feel it. Like an ache at the back of my mind."

"It spoke to you. With words?" Hạc Cúc asked, sharply.

"Just . . . feelings. It was miserable outside of the Hollows, and then it could fly free in the canyon. It was happy in that moment, and it wanted me to be happy, too."

"Destroying everything in the Silver Stream in its path. Some kind of happiness."

Lành slammed her cup on the tray; it took on the blue hue of the energy lines as they diffused heat into it. "I knew you wouldn't understand!"

"No," Hạc Cúc said. It was late and she was tired and she only seemed to have hurtful words left. "You're right. I don't. I'm not the person to come to for absolution. That's not what I do. I kill things. I kill people. I keep people safe. I'm not here to hear excuses about how unreliable you've always been, about why you endangered an entire mission and thought it was fine."

The teacup clattered to the floor. Lành had risen, breathing hard. Her Shadow, unfolding, pressed against Hạc Cúc, trying to push her against the wall—in the heartbeat before Hạc Cúc unfolded her own Shadow, it felt viscous and slimy, and in Lành's eyes pulsed with light on the same frequency as the tangler they had captured. "Take it back," she said. "Take it back!"

"Or what? Are you going to sting me, like the tangler would?"

"I'm not a tangler!"

"You're certainly not giving me that vibe," Hạc Cúc said. She tightened her own Shadow, trying to use Divine Harmony to lift Lành off the floor to make her lose her balance. Lành's Ambush in the Grass effortlessly broke every one of her attempts to seize her. "Is this why my sư phụ rescued you? So you could turn into one of our worst enemies?"

Lành laughed. It was bitter and cutting. "Oh, em. You know why your sư phụ rescued me. Because he's got a heart in his body. Because he's ten thousand times the person you'll ever be. Because you could live myriad lives and die and be reborn myriad times, and you'd still not be him."

Every word was like a knife stab into Hạc Cúc's belly. "Take it back," she said. Her Shadow, wildly weaving, finally struck Lành—lifting her off the ground and sending her flying against the wall.

Lành rolled, catching herself on the energy-fount—for a moment she glowed blue, and then she put a hand on the floor and *pushed*—and all of a sudden her Shadow went from bright, annoying Ambush in the Grass to something dark and viscous. It was holding her against the wall—and Lành pressed again, and the pressure became hard enough to break Hạc Cúc's bones. Hạc Cúc found herself back in the darkness, back with the tangler pressing against her. Back to that viscous touch pushing again and again against her own Shadow, trying again and again to sting her.

She lashed out, pushing back on it—no finesse or technique to her blows, augmented by Shadow. She needed to get free. She needed to break away.

"Chị!" It was Nhi's voice.

Hạc Cúc found herself standing, breathing hard, over Lành. She was on the floor, curled into a ball, Shadow wrapped tight around her. Blood pooled under her hands, and one of her fingers hung at an angle.

She. What had she done?

She.

She hated Lành and everything Lành stood for, but that wasn't a reason—

That—

Hạc Cúc looked up, met Nhi's gaze. In Nhi's face was nothing but stunned horror and repulsion. She raised a hand to her mouth, Shadow flickering into life around her. To protect herself against Hạc Cúc.

Hạc Cúc's stomach heaved.

"That's not who I am," she said. She pinged the inn's owner on her comms, asking for bandages. Then, slowly, shakily, she knelt by Lành's side. "I'm sorry," she said. Lành was conscious, but turned away from her.

That's not who I am.

But Hạc Cúc had seen Nhi's gaze, and she knew. They both knew that this was exactly who she was.

Nhi helped Hạc Cúc bandage Lành, in the light from the energy-fount. They worked in silence. Nhi was still thinking of what to say and do. She'd woken up, woozy and panicked, remembering what she'd worked out when she'd sunk into sleep—and walked to find Hạc Cúc and warn her. Only to find her fighting Lành.

What to do was simple, comparatively speaking. There was a hierarchy of emergencies: in this specific case, making sure Lành was stable was the most pressing task. What Nhi had worked out—the terrible chain of events leading them all here—could wait for a few moments.

Nhi still wasn't sure what to say. Whatever she said in these situations invariably seemed to be the wrong thing, and in this specific case there was so much at stake that she was afraid of messing it up the way she always did. And even if she didn't—she knew too much about Hạc Cúc now. Too many secrets. Too many dark things. It changed things. It always did.

She'd seen Hạc Cúc's face during the fight with Lành—the frozen look and the fear, that rigidity of someone no longer in control. She'd understood then what Hạc Cúc feared: it wasn't just her verbal cruelty, but what it could lead to. A loss of control, such a profound betrayal of everything Hạc Cúc wanted to stand for. She wanted to be perfect. To live up to the potential Quang Lộc had seen in her. And of course Quang Lộc—the legendary Pure Heart Master—would never sink so low as to beat up a fellow junior.

"Here," Nhi said. "She should wake up soon."

Lành's Shadow was like a low-banked fire, but she was still alive. Her eyes were closed.

"Are you—" Hạc Cúc asked.

"I'm not going to say anything," Nhi said. "Not unless Lành's state worsens. Did she start this?"

Hạc Cúc bit her lip. "Maybe she did. But it doesn't change—"

"You're too harsh on yourself."

"No," Hạc Cúc said, sharply. "Would you do the same thing?"

"I'm not you," Nhi said.

Hạc Cúc glared at her, Shadow roiling. "No," she said. "But that's not the point, is it?"

Nhi wasn't really sure why Hạc Cúc seemed so unsatisfied. Why Nhi seemed to make everything worse with everything she said. She fell back to the familiar, the easy. "We need to warn someone."

"You *said* you weren't going to tell anyone," Hạc Cúc said, sharply.

"That's not about this," Nhi said. She could feel Hạc Cúc's anger and shame like physical blows, and wasn't quite sure what to do with either of them. She'd have left, but she couldn't afford to. "It's about the tangler."

"What about the tangler?"

"It's gone."

That was Lành's voice, still thick with unconsciousness.

"Wait. What?"

"It's gone," Lành said. "It was . . . it was free. For a moment only, and then it plunged back."

"Where did it go?"

Nhi forced herself to focus. She accessed the window-screen and changed the view to the canyon where they'd left the tangler. Somehow—even knowing everything that she did—she expected the window-screen to show a pulsing mass of tentacles. She expected to be proven wrong, for her fears to be nothing more than idle fancies. It would have hurt, but it would have been easier to deal with.

But, when the view became clear enough for them to see, there was nothing there. The barrier was gone as if it had never been, and it was just . . . canyon. Buildings. Ruins. Nothing else. Nothing that even suggested there had been a tangler there.

"It *is* gone." Hạc Cúc's face was white. "Where?"

Lành sat up, glaring at them. Her Shadow flickered—it was dark and odd, like it had been before during the tangler chase. "Why would you expect me to know this?"

"Because it *talked* to you!" Hạc Cúc said.

"Stop it," Nhi said. Behind the door, distant noises,

but not the commotion she'd have expected. The moment the barrier went down, surely the elders would have noticed. Surely alarms would have been blaring everywhere. Surely . . . "I need to focus, and this is decidedly not helpful. Plus, that one fight was enough."

Hạc Cúc tensed, Shadow tightening. She'd been hurt by what Nhi had said. Nhi wasn't quite sure why—it was something Hạc Cúc herself would have agreed on—except that obviously, sometimes, people didn't like the implicit made words.

Nhi would have apologized, but she was too busy trying not to panic. "I don't know where the tangler is. But I don't think it went back to the Hollows."

"All right, slow down," Hạc Cúc said. She pointed to Nhi. "*You* weren't going to tell me this about the tangler?"

"No," Nhi said. She looked around her, at the room—and nudged the door closed with her Shadow. She took a deep, shaking breath. "What I was going to tell you is that I don't think we were meant to succeed."

"You make no sense," Lành said. "And why aren't there alarms? If that tangler escaped, we should know about it."

"She does make sense." It was Hạc Cúc, on her other side. "I'd already found it odd, but I'd assumed it was because someone else wanted to look good."

Nhi breathed in shakily. She'd never shied away from the truth, but this truth hurt. "Nebula Cinnabar is a navigator poison, and we already know that none of us poisoned Ly Châu."

"Well, I'm glad to hear we've all been cleared," Lành said.

"Shut up," Hạc Cúc said, sharply. "What of Nebula Cinnabar?"

"You said it yourself. It's a slow poison. Ly Châu didn't get into any fights we saw, didn't get poisoned anywhere in the Silver Stream. Remember when we all met at the Rooster Needle, and she came to pick us up?"

Hạc Cúc inhaled sharply. Nhi could see her hands shaking. "You mean she got poisoned there. Before we ever met her. Back when she was in Rooster territory. The tea," she said, softly. The tea Ly Châu had contemptuously drunk and not shared with anyone else. "But that means—"

That means Elder Liễu had known about it, or closed her eyes on it—or worse, done it herself. "I know what that means," Nhi said, sharply. "I hate it and all it stands for."

"I don't understand," Lành said. She rose on tottering legs, making her way to the door. "You," she said, pointing to Nhi, "make no sense. And you"—she pointed to Hạc Cúc—"assaulted me. I'm leaving. Wherever that tangler is, the elders will catch it. They'll keep us safe. That's what they always do."

She was gone before Nhi could think of anything smart to say. She was . . . not exactly Nhi's friend but at least someone Nhi wished to be well, and she was obviously in distress. "We should find her," she said, slowly. Fix the mess Nhi had made, the words she'd spoken that didn't seem to be the right ones.

"Oh, let her go." Hạc Cúc's voice was dark. "You know what's going to happen if she stays. She'll try to go back to the familiar. Or worse, she'll turn towards the tangler. She can't be trusted."

The same way Hạc Cúc couldn't be trusted to keep calm around Lành? Nhi tried, very hard, to not say the words, because they were true, and hurtful. But she was worried they were showing in her posture—and more importantly, that they were affecting her opinion of Hạc Cúc. "You believe me," Nhi said.

Hạc Cúc was staring at her with a particular hunger in her face. "Always," she said. "Why, though?"

Not why was Nhi saying this, but why the elders were doing this.

"I don't know," Nhi said. "I don't play politics. But, if we'd failed, that tangler would have gone down to the Ice Jade Planet and stung everyone there." She could barely envision the loss of life; it would have been immense. "That we succeeded against all odds"—she saw Hạc Cúc smile at this, briefly—"means they must have set it loose. Which means it's not back in the Hollows. They opened a navigation gate and sent it somewhere."

"Downworld." Hạc Cúc's voice was flat. "That's not a precise enough location."

Nhi shook her head. "It won't be hard to find. Just follow the newscasts for the deaths. Ice Jade is *replete* with habitats. But we'd have to catch it again." It had been difficult enough the first time, and catching it again would just put them back in the same spot. And that they'd have to do it again with too many navigators between them and their target—oh, Heavens. She was going to be sick. Just the thought of having to *talk* to Elder Liễu was making her nauseous.

"Lành could feel it. That's—part of why we had the fight," Hạc Cúc said. "So yes, I think it's loose. I just—we can't just march in there and confront people! We—" She stared at her hands. "I need to contact my sư phụ."

"Ah," Nhi said. "Should I leave?"

Hạc Cúc nodded. "Yes, if you would. I'd rather have the space."

It took an unusually long time for Quang Lộc to answer—time enough for Hạc Cúc to wonder if he already knew about her failure. He couldn't. He was a legend, but even he couldn't possibly have found out. Unless Lành had complained to the Ox Elder and the Ox Elder to the Snake, but surely—

Enough. Anxiety was getting her nowhere.

When he came online, he was looking exhausted. "Hạc Cúc," he said. "What's the matter?"

"It's escaped," Hạc Cúc said. "The tangler. It's. It's loose somewhere, and I don't know what to do."

A silence. Quang Lộc was watching her.

"I did something wrong, didn't I?" She knew what she'd done wrong already, but perhaps there was more. Perhaps there was another test, like the ones he'd used to run in her childhood, the ones where she'd failed and failed until she finally figured out the rules.

At length, he sighed. "I was hoping you wouldn't get involved in this."

Involved. In. This. Her blood instantly ran cold. He couldn't be saying what she thought he was saying. He—

"What is 'this' exactly?" she asked.

Another sigh from Quang Lộc. "You asked me to look into something. I did."

So at least he hadn't been part of it. It was a small and utterly inadequate consolation. "What's going on, Sư phụ?"

"Politics." He looked *old*—not the patriarch, the wise one, just small and tired and like someone she could have snapped in two halves with a mere brush of her Shadow. It was an unavoidable, shameful thought. How dare she have no respect for her sư phụ? "I told you the Dogs were unhappy with the clans."

"Yes?"

"The clans are unhappy, too. They don't appreciate the empire's attempt to cut them out of the navigation business. They feel disrespected. That people have forgotten what it is that they keep away from ships in the Hollows."

Oh, gods. Hạc Cúc said, slowly, carefully, "After we'd tried and failed to catch the tangler, someone was going to look good, swooping in to take all the credit. It was the clans, wasn't it? The tangler was going to get loose in a very large population center, Ly Châu and the Dogs would be conspicuously absent"—being dead did have that disadvantage—"and the clans would just come in and save everyone. But for this to matter, people needed to die first. The risk had to be real." She felt sick to her stomach. "Please—"

"I'm not sure what you want me to tell you," Quang Lộc said.

"Something helpful! Some advice I can use!"

A silence that felt like it was going on for ten thousand years. Quang Lộc said, "I can't help you. You understand that."

No. No. Hạc Cúc didn't. On some level, she did. She'd always known he'd see what she was, how she failed to live up to the promise he'd seen in her. She'd always known that one day, he'd leave, not even turning back to stare at her—because she would no longer be worthy. No, that wasn't it. She'd never been worthy. He'd just have realized she wasn't.

"I don't understand it, no."

A silence. Then, very softly from him, "Then let this be the lesson you never were able to hear from me. You worship the ground I tread on. You think me a living legend."

"Because you are!"

"I'm just a man," Quang Lộc said. "And perhaps once, my cultivation of Shadow was unnaturally good. Perhaps once, I was unnaturally fast when piloting ships. Just as you are."

No. No. No. "You—please—" She was sobbing now.

"I'm just a man," Quang Lộc said. "And in particular, I don't hold any particular power over the elders. I can't stop them."

"You could try!"

"I have tried," Quang Lộc said. "It cost me what little influence I had within the clan. And it didn't work."

"You could—"

"You asked for my advice. My advice to you is this: stand aside."

"Why should I?"

"Because you'll change nothing. Just as I didn't change anything. This'll come to pass, one way or another. And it's better if you're not there when it does." He looked at her. His skin was translucent and thin, and Hạc Cúc saw bones under it, the outline of a fragile, easily breakable skeleton. "You have a future. A bright one. Don't waste it."

"Sư phụ!"

But he'd cut the communication and wouldn't answer, no matter how hard she tried to raise him again.

It was Nhi who found her sprawled on the floor. Hạc Cúc barely heard the door open, but she did feel Nhi's Shadow brushing against hers, a tentative reaching out to her, which she didn't acknowledge. How could she?

"Chị," Nhi said. "Chị."

"I can't," Hạc Cúc said. "I just can't."

"Can't what? What did he say?"

"He said—" Hạc Cúc struggled to breathe. Abruptly Nhi was too close, and she was too vulnerable. Hạc Cúc unfolded her Shadow, pushing herself to stand up. Nhi stood up as well, puzzlement on her face. "He said to stand aside. He said there was nothing to be done."

Nhi stared at her. "And that's what you're going to do? Nothing?"

"What do you want me to do?" Hạc Cúc said.

I'm just a man.

If he was just a man, and she was less than him, where did that leave her? For so long she'd been trying to live up to the example he set; for so long she'd looked up to him as an ideal, while being keenly aware she'd never be him. And now . . .

She was cruel, and he was cowardly, and where did that leave her? Where—

There was nothing that made sense anymore. "I can't," she said.

"Can't what?"

"Remember the bedroom?" Hạc Cúc snapped. "When you couldn't move anymore."

"That's not the same!"

"It is *exactly* the same!"

A silence. Nhi said, slowly, carefully, "I understand you're disappointed. You wanted to live up to an ideal and it turns out to have been rotten—"

"He's not rotten. He's a good man. A good man."

Nhi flinched as if Hạc Cúc had struck her. She took a deep, shaking breath, Shadow slowly hardening around her. "You know he's not a good man."

"No, I don't! You don't know anything." How could she? How dare she judge? How—it wasn't just Quang Lộc she was judging. It was her. Her. Hạc Cúc. The child who'd failed.

A sigh, from Nhi. "You're not him."

"No, I'm not. I'm the kind of person who'll beat Lành bloody just because I can. Just because I'm scared. You know that. You've seen it."

"I have," Nhi said. She didn't say anything more. She didn't need to. Hạc Cúc had seen her look when she'd walked into the room after the fight. The silence stretched on and on, uncomfortable. Because Nhi was too ashamed, too angry at her?

Hạc Cúc should have known what to say, but she could barely move.

The door opened. It was two juniors, one from the Rooster and one from the Ox. "The Elders want to see you."

7

UNSUITABLE COMPROMISES

The juniors took Nhi and Hạc Cúc to the same room in the Rooster quarters where Elder Liễu had received Nhi right after they'd dealt with the tangler. This time, the room was full. The elders were all there: Elder Liễu and the three others. So were the other juniors of their delegation. Bảo Duy was sitting on the floor in front of the elders, still wearing the red hospital gown. She was heavily bandaged and gave the impression that, at any time, she would collapse. Lành straightened up from her bow just as Nhi and Hạc Cúc entered, and took up a position that radiated respect.

The lights had been turned down, the window-screens were off; only the two energy-founts lit up the walls. In deference to Nhi's sensitivities, or to put everyone on their guard?

"Children," Elder Liễu said. "It has come to my attention that we should have kept a better eye on you."

"How did it come to your attention?" Hạc Cúc had knelt, briefly. She looked as bad, or worse, as Bảo Duy. No wonder. The pillars of her world had just collapsed, and she was having to navigate some very difficult waters—and Nhi still didn't know what she could say that would comfort her. Everything just seemed to make it worse. Which was the usual way, wasn't it? People would get angry at her and leave. Too many secrets. Too much vulnerability. Too much tension.

Elder Liễu's gaze flicked to Lành. "I was . . . apprised."

Nhi decided to be blunt for everyone's sake. "Is it true, then?"

"What is true?" That was Elder Ánh Ngọc, the middle-aged plump woman from the Snake that Hạc Cúc seemed to have little reverence for.

"That you set it free," Nhi said.

A sharp breath, from Bảo Duy. Lành's face was unreadable. Nhi waited, stubbornly clinging to what she knew was right.

"Don't question your elders," Elder Ánh Ngọc snapped. "Have your sư phụ taught you no better?"

Elder Liễu raised a hand. "Em," she said, smoothly. "They've displayed admirable resilience and resourcefulness in catching this tangler. Enough, in fact, to no longer be considered juniors. They deserve to know."

A sniff, from Elder Ánh Ngọc. "Have it your way. The consequences are on you, too."

"I'm sure everyone can be reasonable," Elder Liễu said. She threw a peculiar glance at Nhi that Nhi wasn't quite sure how to interpret. Was it a warning?

Nhi was half expecting Hạc Cúc to say something, but she didn't even speak up. It was Bảo Duy who said, carefully, "Nhi is right, isn't she? You set the tangler free. Why—"

"For the future of the clans," Elder Liễu said. The lights dimmed further, and lines of energy sprang between them and the doors, snaking between Nhi's legs. She unfolded her Shadow, drew it tighter to her. If they wanted to categorize that as disrespect, let them. She snuck a glance at Hạc Cúc, whose face was a tumult of emotions.

"You have to understand," Elder Liễu said, "that the Dogs have been pressing us. That there is no respect. That the empire made it so people forget. With each ship that crosses the Hollows safely, the act of navigation is seen as more and more trivial. People who never see a tangler, who are never stung—who never see other people stung—they forget. They forget the skill it takes with Shadow to find the safe passages from navigation gate to navigation gate. To drive the tanglers away. And so they're all the more willing to turn away from us."

"You set the tangler loose. Deliberately." Hạc Cúc's voice was flat. "All of you."

"You—" Nhi swallowed. She'd already worked it all out in her head, but it didn't hurt less. "Did you ask Ninth Judge to find a tangler and crash the ship?" How deliberate had it all been?

Elder Liễu sighed. "They were about to renegotiate the charters. Divert traffic to the Dog Needles for cheaper prices. Cut us out of navigation entirely. What were we supposed to do?"

"Not this!" Hạc Cúc blazed, and she sounded like she was about to cry.

Nhi moved closer to her, but Hạc Cúc's Shadow—roiling and hard—kept her from touching her.

"Now do you understand?"

Surprisingly, it was Lành who spoke. "We're meant to avoid tanglers," she said. She sounded angry and afraid at the same time. Of course. Her worst nightmares made true: the elders working with a tangler.

"You won't have to deal with that tangler ever again," Elder Liễu said, smoothly. "Or would you rather be set to catch it again, knowing you can't kill it?"

Lành stared at her. She mumbled something under her breath, but didn't say anything more aloud.

Bảo Duy pushed herself up from her sitting position with her Shadow—which was pulsing erratically fast, dimming the energy lines in the room as it passed over them. "No," she said. "No one consented to this."

"Ah." The Rat clan Elder—an elderly woman with translucent skin—pursed her lips. "You give us lessons? You and the experiments you ran? All the people you killed, for no gain."

Bảo Duy's face fell. "It was for a good cause. For science. For learning."

"For science." The Rat Elder snorted. "Lines on a ledger. We are talking about the future of the clan, but of course you have never had to understand that, have you?"

With every word, Bảo Duy wilted and folded further into herself, Shadow becoming more and more unstable. "They agreed. The people—"

"The people you killed in your experiments? Did they measure what it was you were asking of them? The risk? The *whole* of it?"

"I couldn't know everything—" Bảo Duy said.

"So no, they didn't consent, did they? And tell me, did the people in this room—your friends—agree, when you took off to see the tangler and left them in the middle of a strobilation with no warning and no defenses? You were the person who knew most about tanglers, the most about defending oneself against them, and you chose to walk away from them."

"That's not the same thing—" But Bảo Duy's voice was low and shaking.

"Of course it is."

"Leave her alone," Hạc Cúc said. She was standing, breathing hard. Nhi didn't like that at all; she knew enough about herself to recognize the same signs of imminent collapse in Hạc Cúc—except she didn't know at all what she could possibly say. She felt as though she was standing on a ship plunging into the Hollows, unable to reach the navigator: she was watching everything happen and she didn't know what to do, the conversation something large and heavy that couldn't be turned back or stopped or even slowed down.

The Ox Elder—the youngest one among them—hadn't said anything so far. She looked at Elder Liễu, and some kind of message passed between them. Elder Liễu said, "You know what your sư phụ would say."

"He tried to stop you!"

A snort, from the Ox Elder. "Is that what he told you? That old man with a quarter of a brain, open to the winds? Of course he didn't. He spoke big words no one understood and then went back to his contemplation." Another snort. "At least when he's cultivating Shadow, it's quiet."

Hạc Cúc took one step back—straight into Nhi, who held her. She disengaged herself, stood on shaking legs. Her Shadow was tumultuous, pulsing again and again against Nhi's hands.

Nhi wanted to say Hạc Cúc's sư phụ wasn't a good man, but that had gone badly enough when it was just her and Hạc Cúc. There had to be something else she could say, but every thought had left her brain.

"He's *respected*," she said. "He's the Pure Heart Master. The one who safely brought the Ten Thousand ships to the Fragmented Shoals Planet during the warlords insurrection. The one who defeated the Silver Fox when she went rogue. He—"

"He's an old man whose time has come and gone," the Ox Elder said. "And you, his disciple." A sigh. "You never did understand how people worked, did you? Never did see past a shell of a reputation. At least Quang Lộc was smart at your age." Her voice was kind, and it just made it worse.

"I'm not broken," Hạc Cúc said, but she sounded like she didn't believe it.

"No," the Ox Elder said. "Your sư phụ is a dotard and you don't even rise to the level he once held. No wonder he wouldn't stand by you."

"Stop it," Nhi said. She didn't know what do anymore, but they were the only words that came to her. "Stop it!"

Everyone stared at her. And not just the Elders. Lành and Bảo Duy—and Hạc Cúc. She saw in their faces—in all their faces—the concern of kind people for someone who was falling apart. She'd spoken too loudly. She looked too disheveled, too distraught, or had the wrong expression on her face. There were some unspoken rules of human interaction she'd failed again, with no idea exactly how.

"This isn't appropriate," she said, but they were still all looking at her.

"Oh, Nhi," Elder Liễu said. "You need rest." And, to everyone: "You all need rest. I suggest you go back to your quarters and use that opportunity." She smiled, but it didn't touch her eyes.

Nhi saw more than felt the Elders leave the room. "We have to stop them," she said.

"Stop them?" It was Lành. "You think we can? You think *you* can?"

Nhi breathed, hard. She was trying to gather some thoughts, to gather some Shadow. Everything felt impossibly far away. "We caught it once."

"And they released it. Be realistic." Lành snorted.

"I'm sorry," Bảo Duy said. Nhi forced herself to look into her eyes, something she did very seldom. There was nothing in them but pity, and that faint look—that realization that something was wrong with Nhi. That it would be better to put distance between the two of them.

And then it was just her and Hạc Cúc. "I just wanted them to stop hurting you," she said, desolately.

Hạc Cúc's face was taut with extreme pain. "They're not the ones hurting me."

"Then who is?" Nhi asked, bracing herself for the answer that would name her.

But Hạc Cúc shook her head. "They're right," she said, tonelessly.

"No!" Nhi grabbed her—and this time Hạc Cúc let her, Shadow folding back. Nhi felt Hạc Cúc's warmth like a shock—on her hands, through her arms. "Nothing they said in this room was right."

Hạc Cúc looked at her. "You don't lie, do you?"

Sometimes she did. "Not to you."

"Then tell me: Did you think they were wrong about my sư phụ?"

Nhi bit her lip. "I don't know enough about your sư phụ—"

"That's equivocation." Hạc Cúc's voice was sharp. "Did you think they were telling the truth?"

Nhi gave the answer she'd been trying to avoid. "No," she said. "But that's not the point. The point is that there's a tangler loose, and that we need to catch it."

Bitter laughter from Hạc Cúc. "Lành is right, and I never thought I was ever going to say that. Even if we catch that tangler again, what are we going to do? Kill it?"

"Bảo Duy can—"

"Not before she does a lot more research. And you and I both know there's no time for this. The elders will find us before that. Are you really ready to go against the clans?"

"Yes," Nhi said. "It's the right thing to do. Aren't *you*?"

A long, exhausted stare from Hạc Cúc. Nhi's heart sank.

"You aren't. Whatever happened to your principles? Your code? To doing the right thing?"

Hạc Cúc jerked back, as if hurt. "The right thing?" She was crying. "My sư phụ is a coward, and I'm cruel. What right thing? What's left?"

"I understand you've had a shock. We've all had a shock—"

"*You* haven't."

Nhi stared at her. "This isn't a competition!" Why was it going wrong?

"No. It's a question of the future." Hạc Cúc stared at her hands. "And they're right. I'm not sure I have any. I'm not sure I ever had any."

Because she wasn't perfect. Because it had all been for nothing. Because, in the end, Quang Lộc had betrayed her, and her clan—who had, by all accounts, never really liked her—hadn't stood by her.

Nhi said, "I believe in you." And, because she had nothing else to say, because it was such a bad thing to say but she'd run out of everything else, because it was the truth: "I love you."

Hạc Cúc's Shadow pulsed, slowly, carefully. "No," she said. "You love an image. A mirage."

That hurt. "You're not going to tell me how I feel!"

A deep breath, from Hạc Cúc. "No, you're right. Then I'll just say this: I can't. I can't return your love. I'm not worthy."

Nhi was shaking now—it was an effort to hold herself together, to hold the light and the noise at bay. "You're impossible."

"And you're naive!!" Hạc Cúc rose, breathing hard. She was surrounded by a dark, agitated mass of Shadow that pushed again and again at Nhi's own Shadow, like repeated knife stabs. "You don't even understand. You take all of your secrets and all of your knowledge and you *judge*."

"I'm not judging!"

"Of course you are. Doing the right thing. Holding us to impossible standards."

"I don't even understand where you're getting that from. You're making absolutely no sense. I—" Nhi was annoyed. She'd made an admission of vulnerability. Several, now. And it was all getting thrown back into her face, and it *hurt*.

Hạc Cúc said, wearily, "You're trying to shame me into going after the tangler. And then you toss love in it like it's a consolation prize. Or another way to make me follow you."

"I'm just—I'm just trying to make you see what you're doing."

"No, you're not." Her voice was sharp, cutting. Her face was hard. Nhi had seen it happen before: that moment when it all snapped. When people walked away and she never really found out why.

"Chị—" she said. "Please—"

"We're done here," Hạc Cúc said. And, in a softer voice, "Find yourself someone. Not Lành, if you can avoid it. Don't fall that low."

And then she left, the same way they had all left—the elders, Lành, Bảo Duy—and Nhi was alone in the room, holding her Shadow close to her until the pressure on her skin was strong enough to impair her breathing—and still finding no comfort.

Nhi snuck out of the inn to get a ship to go down to the Ice Jade Planet and find the tangler.

It was a terrible, terrible plan—she didn't know where the tangler was and she was acutely aware of that fact. But it was either that, or wait in her room for it all to be over. And, if she was being honest, waiting in her room hating herself.

Not for losing Hạc Cúc. That part she had expected—a lot of people in her life eventually left because of things she said.

No, she hated herself for allowing herself to hope. To believe that it could ever be different. That Hạc Cúc would see. Would understand. Somehow. Or that Nhi herself would change, that she'd unlock the ever-shifting and incomprehensible set of rules that allowed her to make sense of other people. To understand why all her appeals to Hạc Cúc had failed, why Nhi's trust and sense of connection, which had led her to share her own secrets—opening her heart—had been utterly mistaken. Or worse—that it had all been going well until she spoiled it.

There were Rooster juniors in the corridors, but they were keeping a bored eye on things. Nhi stepped out of the room, wrapping her Shadow around herself. Her Heavenly Weave was slow and ponderous, and if she angled it right—something she'd done enough, as a child or as an adult in the Hollows—she could make herself seem part of the air around her. It wasn't quite invisibility, but it did prevent people from focusing on her.

The Rooster juniors were bored and not paying attention. They didn't even follow Nhi or raise any kind of alarms as she went down to the inn's reception.

Or so she thought. Because, when she reached the door, Elder Liễu was waiting for her.

"Are you here to tell me to rest?" Nhi said.

Elder Liễu was leaning against the door's jamb. Behind her was the platform where the shuttles waited—where Nhi could probably find her ship and go down to the planet. Elder Liễu wasn't blocking the way, exactly—but she wasn't budging, either. Her Shadow was unfolded, loosely held around her: she didn't expect a fight but she didn't expect this to go well.

The kind of observation that would have been more useful with Hạc Cúc, Nhi thought, stifling the pang of regret. She couldn't afford to think of Hạc Cúc right now.

"No," Elder Liễu said.

"Then why?"

"Because I know where you're going, and I don't want you to die."

"I'm not going to die," Nhi said, and she realized as she said it that she had, indeed, been preparing herself for being stung. Or being killed. Or both.

A sigh, from Elder Liễu. "I should have told you."

Oh. Nhi looked at her. "You sent me with Ly Châu," she said, slowly, carefully. Pieces she hadn't lined up before came together, and she realized something. "You sent me to die once before. That's why you don't want me going again." Not because she thought Nhi was going to make a difference. But out of some misguided idea of how guilt and reparative justice should work. Nhi should have felt hurt. She'd *trusted* Elder Liễu. But she was curiously empty inside. Because . . . because she'd already stepped away from the elders. Seen them as unworthy of respect.

"I didn't. I argued against it," Elder Liễu said.

Nhi was tired, and she'd lost the one person she had felt lately that might make a difference—and she most certainly didn't have the energy to be diplomatic anymore. "As Quang Lộc argued against the tangler plan? He didn't argue very hard."

"You have never understood how it works," Elder Liễu said. "The delicate balance of things in the clans, the compromises we are obliged to make."

"I do understand. A lot better than you think I do," Nhi said. "I just don't think it should come second to what's right."

The grimace Elder Liễu made was eloquent, even for Nhi. "That's exactly what I meant by not understanding," she said. Her Shadow stretched, trying to grab Nhi.

Nhi moved at the last moment, out of its way. "Are you hoping to incapacitate me and keep me in my room?"

"You were ordered to rest."

That wasn't the meaning Nhi gave to rest. The air shimmered, and Elder Liễu moved again towards her, Shadow bumping against Nhi's own—pushing against it, trying to send enough vital energy that Nhi's shield broke. If it did, the resulting shockwave would send her to her knees, and leave Liễu enough time to knock her unconscious.

If there was one thing, however, that Nhi's Heavenly Weave was good at, it was defense. She held her shield, hardening her Shadow, and dodged the next few times that Elder Liễu tried to grab her. Elder Liễu had not expected this; she was growing visibly annoyed.

"You can't stop it," Elder Liễu said. She made a sweeping gesture, a lash of Shadow that almost made Nhi tumble, but she managed to catch her footing at the last minute. "It's already too far away for you to catch. It'd be far better for you if you accepted there's nothing you can do."

Nhi could say and think the wrong thing, but this was unambiguous. "You know where it is," Nhi said. Which meant they'd not just released it, but driven it. With enough Shadow—

Oh, gods.

Another lash from Elder Liễu. Nhi caught it with her hands—feeling the Shadow straining against hers, the rising pressure in her own chest—and pushed. Elder Liễu stumbled.

"Where did you send it?"

Elder Liễu said nothing. She was busy pushing back. Nhi was having to give way little by little, until her back was against one of the tables, the steel digging into it. The owner and the waiters had mysteriously disappeared—which she couldn't blame them for.

"I'm sorry," Elder Liễu said. She raised her hand, palm projecting outwards, Shadow gathering down her arm and wrist. It was one of the techniques her style had been named for—the Blood-Extinguishing Palm. Nhi struggled to get free. "But the sooner the Dogs are out of contention, the better."

Out of contention. Details, mercilessly clear, floated through Nhi's treacherous brain—a desperate attempt to forget a present in which she was about to get knocked out. "The Dog Needle," she said. "It's on the other side of the planet. You can't—"

A sniff, from Elder Liễu. "At least they won't be civilians."

But of course they would be. Dogs might just be the couriers of memorials and imperial news, and there might be the occasional official, but the terminals would be full of people who were looking for these.

Nhi looked up. Above her, the counter held unwashed plates and teacups. She couldn't push back against Elder Liễu, but she could—

"Don't struggle, you're making this harder on yourself."

Nhi gathered her Shadow, and pushed upwards. There was a tearing sound that hurt her ears—and then a clattering of plates. Elder Liễu jolted, then smiled. "That's a poor distraction."

But, for just a moment, her grip had wavered. Nhi launched herself to the side—a fraction of a finger length only, but it was enough to be out of the way of the wave of Shadow that struck the counter, shattering it into chips of molten metal. She raised her own Shadow as a shield—and in that moment when Elder Liễu was out of balance, *pushed* back.

She'd misjudged, or rather, the elder had. She had been

so sure of getting Nhi to comply that she'd barely put up any defenses, which meant that Nhi's own push lifted her and sent her flying into the wall, so hard she made a dent into it.

Nhi stood up, shaking, brushing her clothes. She walked past Elder Liễu—who was still against the wall, looking half-stunned. She made no move to stop Nhi. "This is on you," Elder Liễu said. "Everything that happens."

Everything. Nhi wasn't sure what that was, anymore.

She headed out, towards the tangler—towards whatever little remained of her future.

8

WORTH

Hạc Cúc didn't go far after leaving Nhi. Only to her own quarters, where she tried, with shaking hands, to brew some tea—the lines from the energy-fount didn't seem to connect, in spite of her sending the proper commands. She kept seeing Nhi's face—frowning, disapproving.

Everything she'd thought she knew was in shambles, and in the midst of that, all Nhi could think of was goading her to be worthy of her sư phụ.

Worthy of whom?

She would never be worthy, because there was nothing to be worthy of.

Why had Hạc thought Nhi and she had an understanding? There was nothing there, more of the same drive her former girlfriend had had—being attracted to something Hạc Cúc would never be. The same judgment, and ultimately, it would be the same disappointment—and Nhi would walk away.

No, better to walk away before she was the one who got hurt.

And it had been close, hadn't it.

Because Nhi saying "I love you," for a brief moment, had felt like everything she wanted to hear, water to a parched throat, rice to a stomach stretched with hunger. In a brief moment before it all stung and she remembered what had happened. So she'd lashed out and run.

I love you.

I can't. I can't return that.

And the worst was, it still hurt.

But that was who she was, wasn't it? Unkind. Cruel. Alone.

Hạc Cúc, listless, annoyed at herself, wandered down into the common area of the inn, where she found Bảo Duy playing a solitary game with an encirclement chessboard and some complex rules. Lành was nearby, on one of the couches, doing some Shadow exercises: the lines from the energy-fount lit up the entire couch, so that she seemed to be floating in a sea of light. She raised her gaze when Hạc Cúc came in, briefly nodded at her, and then went back to what she was doing. Bảo Duy wouldn't meet her gaze.

Hạc Cúc sat down at the other end of the couch, and stared at the light. It shifted from the blue of the energy-fount to a deeper, darker color reminiscent of the Hollows.

He's an old man whose time has come and gone.

I'm just a man. Perhaps once, my cultivation of Shadow was unnaturally good.

At least Quang Lộc was smart.

Bảo Duy said, softly, "I feel like we're just killing time until our execution."

A snort, from Lành. "Not ours. We're not the ones who are going to get stung. It'll be the civilians downworld."

"A tangler that size, they won't get stung," Bảo Duy said. "I mean, they will, but it'll progress to death pretty instantly. And it's not going to leave whichever habitat it's devastating. Too much food."

"Thank you for this totally unnecessary and detailed graphic description," Lành said. "It's bad enough sitting here, I didn't need the mental images."

"Perhaps it's what we deserve," Bảo Duy said, uncannily echoing Hạc Cúc's own thoughts.

"For standing aside?" Lành snorted. "What else can we do?"

Hạc Cúc couldn't help it. She said, "Nhi hasn't stood aside."

"Nhi," Lành said, barely looking up from her Shadow exercises, "is weird."

She was not! But Hạc Cúc had been cruel enough, and she wasn't going to pick another fight with Lành. That wasn't who she wanted to be.

"Nhi prefers to be by herself," she said. She held onto the secret Nhi had told her, the one about needing to be alone lest something bad happen—that deep-seated fear of collapse that Nhi always carried with her. Instead, she said, "Because she doesn't always understand other people."

Her gut twisted as she said it. Nhi had said and implied as much, hadn't she? And . . . and she'd tried to comfort Hạc Cúc, in exactly the wrong way. Because she'd misjudged. That was the terrible thing Nhi was afraid of.

And Hạc Cúc—

No, it changed nothing. Nhi was expecting her to be like her sư phụ, or the ideal image she had of her sư phụ, which was worse. She couldn't be those things. Any of those things.

Bảo Duy moved a pawn on the board and sighed.

"We're all weird. That's the reason the elders sent us in the first place. Because they knew we were going to fail."

But they hadn't, had they? In spite of everything that should have doomed them to failure—Lành's bitterness, Bảo Duy's tendency to go off by herself, Hạc Cúc's cruelty and contempt, Nhi's fundamental desire to be alone—they had worked together. They had caught a tangler.

Hạc Cúc remembered what Nhi had told her. *Nothing they said in this room was right.*

Oh, Ancestors.

"We didn't fail," she said, slowly, carefully. Lành looked up. She looked at Hạc Cúc with something like simmering resentment, and no wonder. "We stumbled, but we didn't fail."

"You mean, like what we're doing now?" Lành asked.

Hạc Cúc held up a hand, calling up Shadow. Its feeling—a warmth in her gut, spreading to her arms and then to the outside air—pierced the bubble of doom she'd been wrapping around herself. "Yes," she said. "Because we're choosing to fail."

"You sound like Nhi," Bảo Duy said.

And was that such a bad thing?

She was choosing to be cruel. To lash out. To make herself alone. Just as Quang Lộc was choosing to stand aside.

It was a choice, and she could make a different one.

She said, to Lành, "I'm sorry. I shouldn't have hurt you."

Lành stared at Hạc Cúc as if she'd just drawn down the moon in her lap. "You think that's going to make everything better?"

"No," Hạc Cúc said. "But I was scared and I lashed out,

and that's not who I want to be." She stared at Lành—survivor of a tangler attack, deathly scared of anything and everything that would put her in contact with them, and yet who had still chosen to help. "And everything has to start somewhere."

Lành stared at her, again. Then she folded her Shadow and said, "I'll accept the apology, but don't think it makes us friends."

"Fair," Hạc Cúc said. She said, "I want to go to Nhi. I want to stand with her and stop that tangler. Will you help me?" The pronoun she used was plural.

Lành glowered again. "Picking up your girlfriend? I'm not going along."

"But you agree that what the elders are doing is wrong," Hạc Cúc said.

Bảo Duy began, "They said—"

"I know what they said. They chose the most hurtful thing, and they drove it into our chests." And it had hurt. It had *hurt*. But now her head was clear, and she saw it exactly what it was: a dividing tactic. "There is no moral equivalency between your running out on us and the elders choosing to unleash a tangler on a habitat." She saw it then, clearly. "Not a habitat. They'll unleash it on the Dog Needle. Because that will do the most damage."

Bảo Duy stared at her. She looked sick. Finally she said, "Admit I agree with you. How are you planning to stop that tangler?"

"You said you could kill it."

"Yes," Bảo Duy said. She stared, hard, at the remnants of her game, glimmering in the light. "That was before I saw it, and now that I've seen it, I think it's a miracle the barrier generators can hold it. And it's not going to just go back to the Hollows."

Unbidden, a memory rose in Hạc Cúc's mind. Lành, telling her about the tangler. "Lành?"

"I have a feeling I'm not going to like whatever you're about to say," Lành said. "But I'll listen. Once."

"You said it talked to you."

Lành hissed, as if bitten. "Yes, it did. What of it?"

Hạc Cúc was very careful to keep her voice expressionless. "You said it was miserable outside of the Hollows. You could talk to it. And we could open a navigation gate."

A silence.

Bảo Duy said, "We don't open navigation gates trivially. Because of the risk of tanglers."

Hạc Cúc snorted. "I think that it's too late to worry about that, don't you agree?"

Lành said, "Just to be clear. You're suggesting that I go talk to the stuff of my worst nightmares and try to convince it to go back to the Hollows?"

Hạc Cúc said nothing.

It was Bảo Duy who spoke up, slowly, carefully. "It does make sense."

"All right," Lành said. "Assume it works. Assume we're not stung. Assume we're not dead. How do you prevent the elders from doing the same thing all over again? Let a tangler loose, let it kill Dogs and civilians, use the outcry to sway things in favor of the clans."

"I don't have an answer," Hạc Cúc said. "But this isn't about preventing everything. This is about this one thing that we can affect."

A hard stare, from Lành. "Everything has to start some-where?"

Hạc Cúc swallowed. It still hurt. No magical effect there: Lành could still effortlessly annoy and wound her. But she thought she could understand some of what Lành was doing, and why. She said, finally, "I know you're scared."

"Yes!" Lành said. "Of course I'm scared! You realize what it is you're proposing?"

"Yes," Hạc Cúc said, slowly and softly. And then, equally softly: "It's my ship we'd be using for opening the gate. I'll be piloting it. I know exactly the kind of risk I'm asking you to take, because I'll be taking the same one."

Lành closed her eyes. "I don't understand you," she said. "Why do you think you can suddenly trust me to be anything but who I've always been?"

"That's all you can expect of anyone. And who you are is someone who was scared and still went to place the barrier generators around the tangler."

Lành glared. "You mistake me," she said.

"Do I?" Hạc Cúc held her gaze. It was Lành who looked away, and who said nothing.

Bảo Duy put the final pawn in place and swept the board clean with her hands. The pawns clattered on the floor, one by one—a sound like raindrops on metal. "You're going to need someone to keep an eye on the tangler's behavior while you do this. I can do that. Let's go find Nhi."

"I haven't said yes," Lành said, sharply.

"You haven't?" Bảo Duy shrugged. "What's your an-swer, then?"

For a long while—ten thousand thousands of years in

some court of Hell—nothing happened. Then Lành said, reluctantly, "You understand this is never going to work. But I'm never going to forgive myself if I don't at least try, so I guess that's us, then."

Insofar as battle cries went, this was far from the enthusiasm she'd seen in vids and stories, but Hạc Cúc would take it.

"Let's go," she said.

Nhi's room was empty.
     Oh no.

Hạc Cúc knew exactly why it would be empty, and this was bad, bad news. "She's gone on her own," she said, her stomach twisting.

Lành—whom she'd sent ahead to check if the exits were clear—pinged her from the comms. "Yeah, I know. There's a certain amount of commotion here. Juniors are rushing out, and there's obviously been some kind of a fight near the door."

No no no no. Things had just gone from terrifyingly bad to worse. "Can we sneak out?"

"If you come down right away," Lành said. "It's sheer chaos, I presume because they're trying to catch up to Nhi, but very soon they're going to figure out this specific set of juniors shouldn't be among the people rushing out."

Oh, Nhi. That stubborn, principled, impossible woman—had chosen to head out on her own to try and stop a tangler that couldn't be stopped.

Hạc Cúc felt fear—that very deep-seated terror—that Nhi might be dead before they could get to her.

And there was guilt, too: Hạc Cúc had lashed out at her, and that had been the determining factor in Nhi's isolation. She shouldn't have done that, and yet it might be too late to call it back. Too late to tell Nhi that she did love her, that she did matter. That she did understand.

Hạc Cúc sent up a prayer to ancestors whose effectiveness she wasn't entirely sure of, and hurried down to meet Lành.

Em. Hang on. Please. Hang on.

We're coming.

Nhi was halfway to the Dog Needle when her brain caught up with her. She'd gotten a shuttle with little effort—looking over her shoulder the entire way—and she'd piloted it in her slow, ponderous way, drawing on just enough Shadow to have an idea of where the tangler was without breaking the shuttle. But, as she neared the Dog Needle, the trail of the tangler bumped into her Shadow— and she felt it become denser and denser, a viscous mass that didn't care much for her existence or her desperate and futile attempts to stop it.

It felt bigger, larger than when she'd first seen it. Had whatever happened with Lành made it larger? Or had the clans fed it before releasing it?

The thought was like a sharp prickle that she couldn't get rid of. She was a junior without permission to have her own ship—she'd only piloted Rooster clan ships on her rare outings. She hadn't expected much of life—not even a rise to full-blown navigator. But she'd believed, in spite of all available evidence, that navigators were *decent*.

That belief had obviously been mistaken, and now she

was having to reassess rather a lot of things about her life. Or whatever was left of it.

Nhi didn't see any of the clan navigators. Presumably they'd left after doing the deed. Wait.

She turned, staring at her sensors. Yes, there were dots that didn't quite rise above the threshold for full-blown detection. Far too many ships and far too organized. The navigators were behind her. Either the ones who'd driven the tangler there or the ones Elder Liễu had sent after her.

Either way, she wasn't alone.

Ahead was the Dog Needle: this far away, it was just a sliver of steel, glinting against the blue-grey layer of clouds that covered the Ice Jade Planet. Behind her, somewhere barely visible, was the Silver Stream, the Fragments of the broken moon. Nhi had barrier generators in her hold, and not much else. She was too far away from either to expect anything—and in any case, who would stand with her?

In the end, she'd always known that she'd be alone because the secrets she held had driven everybody else away.

Well, there was nothing for it.

Nhi put the shuttle on a straight course for the Dog Needle, and descended into the hold to find a suit and a glider.

The upper atmosphere wasn't quite like the Old Rise, and neither suit nor glider had been meant for it. Nhi could feel the friction that was slowing down the glider, and despite the suit, she was feeling frozen to the bones: the wind was getting into it. She sent a burst of Shadow onwards— and in the brief layer of darkness it created, she saw the outline of so many tendrils.

It was *huge.*

Breathe. Breathe. She set her suit to muffle outside sounds—it wouldn't do to have a crisis due to oversensitivity.

She couldn't kill it or trap the tangler, but maybe, maybe, she could divert it from the Dog Needle, and make it head towards somewhere where it'd be less likely to do any damage.

Nhi deliberately didn't think about what was going to happen next, because diverting the tangler was only postponing the problem. She needed to be doing something, anything.

She dived to the side, raising Shadow around her.

She almost immediately felt the stingers, and they weren't randomly moving. The tangler was aware of her, and it was moving to—assimilate her? Sting her? Eat her? She wasn't quite sure. She hardened her Shadow against the pressing onslaught of viscousness.

On her comms, a ping, then another. "This is the Rooster clan. Stand down! We'll come to retrieve you."

And another familiar voice: Elder Liễu's, pleading. "Nhi, please. Don't make this any harder on yourself."

Alone.

Forever alone.

It was a choice of the tangler and her ideals, or admitting defeat and going back to the clans—and there was no question as to what her answer would be. Nhi clamped herself as tight as she could to the glider, and accelerated, straight towards the mass of tendrils.

They wrapped around her, as if they were a second shield to match the one she was already raising—except she felt the pressure of the stingers, the viscousness, as if algae were trailing again and again against her Shadow, chipping away bits and pieces of it in the process. Her chest burnt, and she was already shaking with the effort of holding against the tangler.

Nhi took a deep breath, and steeled herself for the end.

9

THE DOG NEEDLE

Having people on board *The Steel Clam* was weird, but not as weird as having Lành sit next to her and feel almost no urge to be unkind to her. It wasn't that Hạc Cúc had lost her bad habits that fast but rather she was navigating quickly and aggressively while trying to keep her mind clear of worrying about Nhi.

Come on, come on, come on. Please hold out, em. Please be there.

The ship was pure clan: it was reinforced, mobile, maneuverable, and being back on board was like breathing again. Unlike everything else she'd piloted so far, this felt like an extension of her will. She *scythed* through the atmosphere, Shadow extended around her—Divine Harmony, fast, aggressive, stealthy, the way she'd always been meant to be—except that her thoughts were full of worry for Nhi.

Come on, come on.

"I can feel it," Lành said.

Ahead on the window-screen, a glint above the cloud layer: the Dog Needle, so far away she could barely see its infrastructure. There would be ships if she went closer, and shields of Shadow, but even the long-range sensors couldn't quite feel them yet. "Can you feel how far it is from the Needle?"

"It's not that precise, no. All I know is that it's some-where, and we're getting close."

"How—" Hạc Cúc tried to find a tactful way to broach the question while steering a ship at breakneck speed through the upper atmosphere. They were high enough that there was an atmospheric tide—a messy, messy prospect with the Fragments of the broken moon doing weird things with gravity—and she was currently having to push against the overall direction of said tide. "How is it feeling?"

"Puzzled. Angry," Lành said. She didn't sound happy. "It was imprisoned, and then they let it out, and it grew larger because it fed?"

"It fed on what."

"I think one of the Ox juniors' shields slipped when let-ting it loose," Lành said. "Please don't ask me to speculate any further."

"I'm good," Hạc Cúc said. "I'm firmly in favor of the contents of my stomach remaining in my stomach."

Please be alive, em. Please hang on. Please please please.

She'd half expected Bảo Duy to weigh in, but her only answer was a distant grunt on the internal comms. She wasn't on the control deck. She was down in the belly of the ship, in the hangar, busy doing something to one of the gliders. She'd asked Hạc Cúc for permission, and Hạc Cúc had granted it. She could always replace gliders. She couldn't resurrect Nhi, and the thought of being in that po-sition hurt worse than the thought of a tangler's sting.

There were *ships* ahead of them. Navigator ships. Hạc Cúc swore under her breath. "They're chasing her."

Lành pursed her lips. "Can I say something you're not going to like?"

"Yes," Hạc Cúc said. The atmospheric tide was moving, which was annoying. It was taking everything she had to keep the ship moving fast. The atmosphere was pushing against her Shadow, and it felt as though she was continually having to push back. It exhausted her, and she could feel her inner strength draining.

"It might not be the worst thing if they're chasing her," Lành said. "Surely they'd retrieve her before she got stung by the tangler."

Bảo Duy said, from the hold, "We're talking about people who thought dead Dogs and dead civilians were an acceptable price to pay for the continuation of the clans' hold on commerce."

"Precisely," Hạc Cúc said. She gritted her teeth, refusing to voice her worst fear aloud. That they'd let Nhi die in a heartbeat, because they thought she didn't matter. Or worse—that Nhi would let herself die, through a combination of principles and thinking she mattered less than them.

The dots of the clans' ships were getting larger and larger. Time to fight.

"Get ready," she said.

Lành got up and left the control deck to join Bảo Duy in the hangar. After a while, Hạc Cúc saw the hangar doors open, and two dots of light—two gliders—slip out of the ship.

"We need a distraction," she said.

"Yes, that's you," Bảo Duy said. Her voice sounded muffled. Hạc Cúc could feel, distantly, her Shadow getting further and further away from the ship's hull.

"I need to open the gate." She was the only one who

could; it was possible to do it on a glider—it would require control—but no glider would be able to withstand the pull into the Hollows, and no person in a suit and a glider could be expected to survive in the Hollows.

"We'll get to that bit later," Bảo Duy said, sharply. "Right now, I need you to distract them so Lành can talk to that tangler, and also to find where Nhi is."

Hạc Cúc opened her mouth to protest, closed it. Bảo Duy was right. One thing at a time.

She extended her Shadow, softening it until it merged with the ship—until it was the atmosphere and the tide and the gravity of the broken moon, until everything was her and she was everything.

And then she dived towards the waiting clan ships, with the same ruthlessness and drive she had on her clan missions—when she moved in for the kill; when her targets saw her coming and knew it was too late to stop her.

They scattered in shock, like a flock of scared birds. It wasn't going to last. Any moment now, they'd realize it was a junior's ship, a junior's Shadow and technique—and then, if there was an elder on board, they'd regroup.

"I can see her!" Bảo Duy's voice was sharp. "She's— she's in the middle of the tendrils. That's not good."

Everything froze. There was nothing left but rage in Hạc Cúc's mind. "Don't you dare," she said, on the comms to those fleeing clan ships. "Don't you dare kill her." It was only after she'd spoken that she realized she'd just threatened the entire Council of the Eight where everyone could hear her.

Silence. A faint buzzing of sound. Then Elder Liễu's shaking voice, "We're not trying to kill her."

Lành's voice, floating on the comms. "I'm almost close

enough." She'd unfolded her Shadow: her Ambush in the Grass was dark and pulsing, with that same weird viscousness to it, nothing human, nothing clan. She was on the left side of the tangler, going closer to the umbrella, Bảo Duy in lockstep behind her. "Give me a moment."

"I can see her," Bảo Duy said, again. "She's not going to hold on for very long. If Lành can do something—"

"Lành would like to be left alone," Lành said, grimly and with a voice that felt like it belonged in the Hollows—echoing, words slurred. "So I can talk to this—thing. It's very eager to have some company, and I'd rather it didn't try to sting me."

So, a distraction, then.

Hạc Cúc could provide that. In spite of the way her heart was in her throat—in spite of her fears for Nhi, her anger at herself and everyone else complicit with this situation—she could do that.

She opened her comms, trying to find the frequency for Nhi. "Em!" she said, sharply. "Em." And to Elder Liễu, slowly and savagely, "Stand aside. Now."

And she reached deep inside for her Shadow—to make herself seem bigger than she was, hoping to scare them all into action.

Nhi was failing. She was falling. The shield of Shadow she'd deployed was getting thinner and thinner, the tendrils she couldn't see pressing against it. Her entire body was going limp because all her energy was maintaining the faltering shield, and it was only the magnetic clamps that kept her attached to the glider. She was scared, but it was almost soothing. They'd stopped trying to reach her; she'd stopped having to make an effort.

She was alone and it was going to be horrible, but at least it was going to be quick.

Her comms were beeping. She ignored them. People had stopped saying things that made sense some time ago.

Almost gone.

And then she felt it. An effusive and fast series of—not blows, but pushes. She knew that Shadow, that technique.

Bảo Duy?

"Em!" It was Hạc Cúc.

Wait.

They'd walked away. All of them. They'd left her, after she'd said—she didn't know what. But she'd said it, and everyone had looked at her with pity in their eyes, and they'd left her. To the tangler. To Elder Liễu.

People left. They didn't come back. "Chị? Em?"

"We're here." Hạc Cúc's voice was thick with relief.

Back. They were back. No one had ever come back for her. Nhi struggled to breathe. "What—"

"We're here," Hạc Cúc said, again. "Hold on just a little longer, please. Em."

A flood of relief.

"Please. Hold on."

They had come back. She wasn't alone. She had them. She had Hạc Cúc.

Hạc Cúc.

"Chị," she said, on the comms. "I—" She wasn't quite sure what she wanted to say. Some admission of vulnerability, of love?

"Shh. I know. Now isn't the time," Hạc Cúc said. She sounded relieved, but also under some huge strain. "Let's get you out of there, and then we can talk. Promise."

"Promise?" She sounded so garbled, so incoherent. But she wasn't alone anymore, and it was like a warmth in her belly.

"Promise."

"I'm close enough." Lành's voice, on the comms. Her Shadow spreading. And then her voice again, but this time it wasn't speaking human words. It was saying syllables that echoed around in Nhi's brain, things that stretched like wax, without significance or logic.

"Em." It was Hạc Cúc, on a private channel. "We're going to get you out of there."

"How?"

Around her, something shook. The tendrils. They were pulling away. "How—?"

"Don't ask questions." Hạc Cúc's voice was darkly amused. "You really don't want to know."

A glider nudged hers. Hands held her. "I have her." It was Bảo Duy.

"Chị," Nhi said, or tried to say. It all came out jumbled.

"It's all right," Bảo Duy said. "We're getting you out, and then we're going to need to move fast."

"You're making no sense." It still came out jumbled, but Bảo Duy's grip on her didn't waver.

"We're here," Hạc Cúc said. As Bảo Duy pushed out of the mass of tendrils—the tendrils that had spread to let them pass—as Lành spoke words that Nhi couldn't understand, frequencies that vibrated in Nhi's muscles and teeth, Nhi saw the ship waiting for her and felt, distant and relieved, Hạc Cúc's Shadow, waiting to wrap itself around her. To hold her.

"We're here," Hạc Cúc said.

Here. *I love you*, she tried to say, but the words wouldn't get past her exhaustion, and anyway, it had gone so badly the last time she'd tried them. "Chị—I."

"Shh," Hạc Cúc said. "I know. It's all right. We've got you." And, softer still, like a wholly inadequate answer to the words that Nhi had not been able to utter, "I am here, em."

On the comms, Lành was speaking that strange language again. Hạc Cúc was trying, very, very hard, not to do anything lacking in common sense—like running away as far as possible, or going straight for Nhi so she could hold her. Instead she was swooping and diving, Shadow extended, scattering the clan ships. They were extending Shadow now—it was Elder Liễu's style, the Blood-Extinguishing Palm, a fighting style that sent thin, sharp jolts of Shadow into the atmosphere, each strong enough to badly damage a ship's engines.

Hạc Cúc dodged. Again and again. Her Divine Harmony style didn't include much in the way of shields. She usually swooped in, stabbed people as hard as she could with blades of Shadow, and then swooped out and ran fast.

That was obviously not going to work in this situation. She didn't have stealth, which was a prerequisite. She wasn't the strongest one—that would be the Elder—and above all, she was hopelessly outnumbered, and it was taking all her focus just to keep her ship moving. She'd got Nhi out of trouble, but she wasn't sure they could pull off the rest.

It was going to take a small miracle to get out of this.

As they cleared the tangler's last tendrils, Nhi was able to pull herself into a semblance of being upright, or at any rate no longer limp. It wasn't much—she was exhausted, and every noise seemed a little too loud in a way that prefigured total collapse—but it was something.

She could see, far away, the Dog Needle. And, much closer, clan ships—weaving, dodging, running. Shadow deployed—shockwaves that she felt the distant echo of. She unfolded her own Shadow, held it close even though it was shaking.

One of the ships was diving, again and again, towards the others, aggressive and fast, extending Shadow seamlessly. It was a clan ship, and—

Oh.

That was Hạc Cúc, wasn't it? She was distracting the ships. To Nhi's eye, it was obvious that it wasn't a fair fight, but Hạc Cúc's ship looked threatening enough that no one—not even Elder Liễu—wanted to engage.

"Are you going to be all right?" Bảo Duy asked.

"I—I think so," Nhi said. She'd always been good at processing and compartmentalizing information. That she'd almost died was a thing she'd deal with later; right now, it was obvious that the present needed her, and needed her fast.

"Good." Bảo Duy's voice was warm. Nhi wasn't sure how to take it. They'd come back. The enormity of what had happened was a little too much, a little too raw. "I need to keep an eye on the tangler for Lành, and my glider got damaged a bit."

"How badly damaged?" Nhi asked.

Bảo Duy made a noise that was noncommittal. "I can

function. I'm just going to keep well away from anything that requires maneuvering."

"You said you needed to watch Lành?" Nhi could see Lành. She was on the glider, standing with her feet firmly planted where the magnetic clamps were. Her head was raised towards something Nhi couldn't see, and everything about the pose spoke of reverence.

"Not Lành, the tangler. Just to make sure it's not trying anything funny. Lành is trying to convince the tangler to go home. Then Hạc Cúc is going to open a gate." Bảo Duy's glider pulled away from Nhi's. "Can you get to Hạc Cúc's ship? Or at least keep your head down."

And then she was gone. Nhi held on to her glider, hanging from it like some dark and awkward fruit. She watched Hạc Cúc dive again and again, dodging the blasts of Shadow from Elder Liễu's Blood-Extinguishing Palm. She shivered. She could feel the pull of the atmospheric tides on her suit; with the motor off, she was drifting further and further away from the battle.

She turned on the motor, feeling the low rumble of it—a little too much, a little too loud for her overstimulated sense of hearing. She nudged the motor into a higher speed so the inertia made her horizontal again, dragged along by the glider once more.

So. A gate. It made sense. Getting the tangler back to the Hollows was the fastest way to get rid of it. But it presumed some ability to herd it, which they didn't have. The clans had probably set it towards the Dog Needles, but that would have taken a lot of juniors and elders working together. And ships.

Which they didn't have.

They had the one ship, and Hạc Cúc on board it.

Think think think. Nhi watched Hạc Cúc dodge again and again. She stared at the evidence, holding everything together in her mind: Lành's fear of tanglers, Bảo Duy's broken glider and her tendency to hold her life too cheap, Hạc Cúc's single-mindedness.

She was currently the only one with the capacity to do anything.

Nhi reached for their shared comms channel. Lành was speaking, her words echoing as if under a large ceiling. There was something odd and vaguely disturbing about each syllable, something Nhi couldn't quite put her finger on. "It's unhappy, but it's not going to change course. It doesn't believe we can fix anything. No one has fixed anything for it."

Ah. Nhi knew how that felt all too intimately, and that it was a tangler having those doubts didn't change the solution much. "You have to open the gate now. In front of it."

"What? No."

"It doesn't trust us because we haven't done anything except trap it behind barrier generators. Open the gate, and it'll see that we mean what we say." Something far too few humans did anyway.

"I can't open a gate now," Hạc Cúc said, grimly. "Mostly because my attention is engaged elsewhere." Something clattered, in the background. Hạc Cúc hissed.

"Are you all right?" Nhi asked.

"Ask me again when we're done," Hạc Cúc said.

A deflection. Nhi hoped Hạc Cúc was all right.

Still . . . still, it was obvious, and it would have been obvious to all of them, except that Lành was stressed because she was communicating with the stuff of her nightmares, Bảo Duy was too worried Lành would die, and Hạc Cúc too busy keeping the clans at bay from them.

"You're not going to be able to open a gate," Nhi said.

"You just told us we had to!" Bảo Duy's usually calm voice was strained.

"I mean *you're* not," Nhi said. "Opening a gate requires concentration and stability. Hạc Cúc is too busy fighting off the clans, and even if she did break off from them, they would chase her. Bảo Duy's glider is broken. And Lành is keeping the conversation open with the tangler."

A grunt, from Lành. "Please do something fast. Not going to last long here."

"You're not making sense," Bảo Duy said.

"You can't open a gate," Nhi said. "But I can."

Hạc Cúc spoke, sharply. "No," she said. "You're not, em. I forbid it. We didn't do this whole rescuing of you just so you could endanger yourself again."

Nhi smiled. "Opening a gate doesn't require a ship."

"But it does require a ship to not get sucked into it!"

"Ah." Nhi smiled, with a lightness she didn't feel. "How fast are you, chị?"

"You're asking me to pick you up." Hạc Cúc's voice was flat. "In front of a gate that you just opened."

"They did say you were the fastest and best pilot of your generation."

"I think," Hạc Cúc said, coldly, "you have me confused with my sư phụ."

And wasn't that a sore spot? But before Nhi could say anything, Hạc Cúc spoke again on a private channel. "Sorry," she said. "I allowed my emotions to get the better of me. Tell me, genuinely: Do you think that's the only way to do this?"

Nhi chewed on it for a while. She said, at last, "Bảo Duy can't maneuver enough. Lành is too scared. And you're too busy."

"And too busy to pick you up?"

"You know, and I know, that opening and holding a gate open requires focus that piloting a ship doesn't. And once the gate opens, every single clan ship is going to be very confused about what's happening and why. You'll have an opening. It won't be large, but you'll have one."

A sigh, from Hạc Cúc. "I don't like this."

"I'm not asking you to like this," Nhi said. "Because I don't like it either. I'm asking you to trust me. It's different."

The conversation they weren't having hung in the air.

I love you.

I can't return that.

But she had come back.

A silence. Then, on the open channel, Hạc Cúc's steady voice: "I do trust you, em. Let's do this."

A re you in position?"

"Not yet," Nhi said. She'd pushed her glider as fast as it could go, trying to make for that space in front of the tangler. Behind her, the clan ships were too busy engaging with Hạc Cúc—who was doing a stellar job of keeping them distracted. "Almost."

Hạc Cúc had promised that she could disengage from them fast enough to pick up Nhi, and Nhi would have to trust that, too.

"I'm here," she said.

There was no tangler—it was at her back, a thick and viscous presence she could feel, the thing that had almost killed her. It wasn't nearly as scary as it should have been, because it was just a creature. A thing that did what it had to do to survive, and the scariest ones were the people. The clans. The elders. Those who would casually sacrifice others.

"Are you ready?" Nhi asked.

Ahead was the glistening of the Dog Needle: the barely visible ships taking off, landing, the same dance as the Rooster Needle, something that, in spite of everything, remained a comfort. A reassurance that the world moved on as it always did.

Nhi moved into position, maneuvering her glider to be steady.

"I'm ready," Bảo Duy said.

Lành broke off, briefly, from the incomprehensible language she was speaking on the comms. "I've told it we're opening a gate. It's waiting," Lành said. They'd both moved away from where Nhi was, far enough that they wouldn't risk being caught in the pull of the open gate.

"I'm ready to catch you," Hạc Cúc said, and Nhi felt a treacherous warmth in her belly.

Opening a navigation gate was like stabbing oneself in the gut. To Nhi, it felt like the entire universe was tearing itself apart. As Lành continued to speak that incomprehensible language, she felt her Shadow widen and stretch, and then drain away, siphoned into the enormous amount of energy it took to connect with the Hollows.

Ahead of her, a hole appeared, and grew and grew. Within, it shimmered—an iridescence halfway between pearl and oil, which then became distorting pinpoints of light, a window into the weirdness of the Hollows. Outside, the air felt charged, a storm of swirling tension, drawing Shadow into its center, where it burst into myriad fragments that distorted the light further.

Nhi felt the pull of that gate: it was drawing in her Shadow and drawing her in, too, pulling at the places where her Shadow was born—the meridians in her body, the vitality center in her lower belly, at the intersection with the lines of her perineum. Like a tide, it caught her and her glider and drew her in—and unlike a tide she was powerless to resist it.

Chị . . .

"I can't hold it—"

"Lành?"

A pause. Lành's speech wavered. "Almost there," she said. "Keep it open just a little longer. It wants to go home." And there was bright and terrible longing in her voice.

The longing would have been concerning if Nhi hadn't been doing her utmost to not get sucked into the Hollows. "I can't—"

Something large—like wings unfolding, like the cloth of Heaven stretched around her—an unbreakable hold of Shadow that caught her and held her and dragged her back, never wavering, never letting go, a steady, unwavering grip that felt like it was her entire world.

"I've got you, em," Hạc Cúc's voice said.

Lành spoke again. And then the universe tore itself apart again. Something rippled. Against Nhi's Shadow, the tangler *slid*—diving straight into the open maw that she was holding open. Nhi felt it, all of it—umbrella, tendrils, stingers—

and then it was gone, and Hạc Cúc's Shadow was pulling her into her ship, and she could finally breathe again.

Hạc Cúc's focus was shot. Some of it was on Nhi—who was making her way from the hangar floor to the control deck—some of it was on the clan ships, who were milling uncertainly among themselves, and some of it was on Lành and Bảo Duy.

She snapped, to Lành, "That tangler is going home but you're not. Lành? Can you hear me? You're not going with it!"

The gate closed. It felt as though something had been cut loose: the terrible pull that Hạc Cúc had been trying to hold at bay was no longer there, and it felt like she could finally breathe again.

The clan ships were diving towards Hạc Cúc. She dodged them, but her Shadow felt spent. The tension and effort of the last few moments had finally drained it. Far away—further away, beyond the gate, ships were lifting from the Dog Needle, coming towards them. It was too big a disturbance.

"Your concern is touching," Lành said, on the comms. "But I'm not going away quite that fast."

Hạc Cúc let out a breath she hadn't been aware of holding.

"We're headed back to your ship." Bảo Duy was the only one who seemed unshaken.

"Chị?" It was Nhi, standing at the door of the control deck. Shaking, pale, but whole. A surge of profound, violent relief went through Hạc Cúc. "It's gone," Nhi said. "We did it."

Hạc Cúc wanted to run to her and hug her, but there were pressing concerns. Nhi made her way closer to her, and stood there, Shadow against Shadow.

"I'm so glad you're here," Hạc Cúc said.

Nhi smiled, and it did weird things to Hạc Cúc's insides when she did. She held out her hand, and Nhi took it.

"Chị!" It was Lành. "I guess you're both probably having a well-deserved but entirely misplaced moment of intimacy, but could you do something about those clan ships? Please?"

Clan ships.

Hạc Cúc stared at the ships approaching from the Dog Needle. She was having to lean against a chair to keep her balance and was keenly aware that whatever Shadow she had left wasn't strong enough, and certainly wouldn't withstand a frontal attack from Elder Liễu's ship. She thought of Ly Châu and the clans, and of Lành's question, about what would prevent the elders from doing this again.

Nothing from within the navigator clans. But the clans weren't the only ones with a stake in this. "Yes," she said. "I can absolutely do something about those clan ships." And she flicked a switch, steeling herself to hail the Dog ships.

10

AFTERMATH

The Dogs were not happy, but there were enough of them that the clans had to back down.

They transferred the four of them to private holding rooms on the Dog Needle, and questioned them. Extensively. By the time it was finally settled—by the time angry negotiations were being opened with the major clans, and demands for reparations were being made, Hạc Cúc had lost what little stomach for diplomacy she'd ever had.

No blame was attached to them. Lành had very creatively fudged around her own role in convincing the tangler. Hạc Cúc couldn't blame her.

Still, the fact of the matter remained: none of them were welcome in the clans anymore. They'd known it, in a way, when they'd decided to go after the tangler, but it didn't make it any less difficult to deal with.

Late one night, Hạc Cúc went to have the conversation she'd been avoiding.

Nhi was sitting in her bed in her room, watching the window-screen: she'd had it display the Central Rooster Needle, so she was watching a ballet of traffic that she must have watched all her childhood. A comforting, familiar sight she couldn't go back to.

"I came to apologize," Hạc Cúc said.

Nhi raised her gaze from her bandaged hands. "For what?" she asked. "For coming to get me?"

"For hailing the Dogs," Hạc Cúc said.

"Is that what you're here to do?" Nhi asked. Her voice was sharp. "Really?"

Hạc Cúc sighed. She sat on the bed. "No," she said, finally. She stared at the energy-fount, trying to find words. "I did promise we would talk. I shouldn't have pushed you away. I know I came back. I know we came back."

"You convinced everyone to come back." Nhi's voice was sharp again.

"That's not the point!" Hạc Cúc took a deep, shaking breath. "You offered me something. Something that was yours. And I threw it in your face. I almost got you killed."

"Ah." A silence. Nhi stared at her lap. "You came back." There was wonder in her voice. "People don't, usually."

"And that's the bar you have for people? That they get angry at you, abandon you, and then come back? It's *wrong*. You shouldn't be abandoned," Hạc Cúc said. She breathed in, slowly, steadily. "I'm sorry. You were trying to say things, and I couldn't listen to them."

Another sigh from Nhi. "I know what you're trying to say. Or rather, I'm not sure. Are you trying to pick another quarrel because you don't think you're worthy?"

Hạc Cúc grimaced. "Maybe," she said. "Or maybe not." She thought of Quang Lộc and of Lành, and of all the ways in which they could fail each other. "Mostly I'm thinking that sometimes you're very sharp and sometimes people make no sense to you, and that you are beautiful just the way you are."

Nhi breathed in, sharply.

"Did I hurt you?" Hạc Cúc asked.

"Surprised me, that's all."

"I did hurt you, before." Hạc Cúc took a deep breath, and bodily flung herself into the void. "I love you. Just the way you are," she said. She was going to add something about not deserving it, but she stopped herself just in time. "I want to be with you. If you'll have me. We can go somewhere away from this all. On my ship."

A silence. Then soft laughter, from Nhi. "If I'll have you? Sometimes you're the one who doesn't understand people, you know that? Of course I will have you. What do you think I've been waiting for?" And Nhi bent over and kissed Hạc Cúc, slowly and deeply—and it felt like coming to a home she hadn't realized she needed.

It felt right, to kiss Hạc Cúc. To have that warmth on her lips—but, more than anything else, what felt right was the truth that Hạc Cúc had said. That there was nothing wrong with Nhi or with the way she was. That it wasn't she who drove people away. It was the people who left who didn't deserve her.

And that, in the end, Nhi had found someone who would not just come back for her, but who would stand with her.

As Nhi and Hạc Cúc were on the threshold of Hạc Cúc's ship, Lành's voice stopped them.

"Where do you think you're going?" she asked.

"Checking a few things out," Hạc Cúc said, smoothly.

Nhi held Hạc Cúc's hand, still trying to get used to its warmth.

"You mean leaving without us," Bảo Duy said.

"What are you going to do?" Nhi asked.

Lành rolled her eyes upwards. "Heaven knows," she said. "It's not exactly like we're going to be welcome among the clans anytime soon."

Nhi stared at Bảo Duy, and then at Lành—and then at Hạc Cúc. She suddenly realized—and it was a shock—that Hạc Cúc wasn't the only one who wanted to be with her.

"Chị," she said.

Hạc Cúc sighed. "It was an offer for two," she said, but she didn't sound wholly convinced herself.

"You did get us here," Nhi said. "Calling the Dogs. Getting us thrown out of the clans."

"That's not fair. We all got here," Lành said. "Jointly. Remember? It was a decision we all made, to walk away."

Bảo Duy sighed. "I don't know that it was the right thing to do. No more experiments."

"You can try and talk the Dogs into them," Lành said. She sounded sarcastic, but it was almost affectionate.

"I'd rather not deal with the Dogs for now," Bảo Duy said. "So?"

She looked at Hạc Cúc. Hạc Cúc sighed, theatrically. "Fine," she said. "Fine. You can come with us. But I'm piloting, at least until you figure out how not to kill us. Or crash this ship."

Bảo Duy grinned. "I'll pack."

Lành and Hạc Cúc stared at each other, until Nhi was worried that she'd have to intervene. But then Lành said, slowly and grudgingly, "You understand that I still don't like you."

Hạc Cúc snorted, Shadow unfolding. "Same here."

"Good," Lành said. "So long as that's clear, I'll go get my things."

When they were gone, Nhi looked at Hạc Cúc. The idea of having people with her was unfamiliar and somewhat uncomfortable—but not unwelcome. "Do you think they'll let us?"

"Let us do what?"

"Ferry people."

Hạc Cúc chewed on it for a while. "Rogue navigators? I think everyone—the Dogs, the clans—is going to be quite busy dealing with each other in the near future to worry about what four juniors are up to."

"It's weird," Nhi said.

"Yes," Hạc Cúc said. "You can still decide you'd rather not have it."

"Any of it?" Nhi asked.

Hạc Cúc looked worried for a moment. Nhi laughed. "I didn't mean you. Come here."

She drew Hạc Cúc close and kissed her—and their Shadows softened and mingled with each other. And Nhi knew that whatever happened in the future, she would no longer have to bear it alone.

ABOUT THE AUTHOR

ALIETTE DE BODARD writes speculative fiction, and has won three Nebula Awards, an Ignyte Award, a Locus Award, and six British Science Fiction Association Awards. She is the author of *A Fire Born of Exile*, a sapphic *The Count of Monte Cristo* in space, and of *Of Charms, Ghosts and Grievances*, a fantasy of manners and murders set in an alternate nineteenth-century Vietnamese court. She lives in Paris.